SWING HIGH SWEET HARRIET

BY

BARNEY HIGGINS

All rights reserved, copyright 2023 by Bill Magill

PART ONE
The Seven Stars public house

Take the woke warning as read.
Hold on to your hats.

LUSHOUS LOUISE   I now find that blackmailing small timers like you, Higgins, is below my dignity.

  [I can see her point. She's built for better things]

BARNEY   And who shall be your next victim, it that's not a rude question
  [say I, asking a rude question]

LUSHOUS LOUISE   Oh, you do look funny.

BARNEY   So would you if you were hanging upside down.

Enter THE CRUSHER   Hang on there, Barney, I'll save you.

BARNEY   Untie the rope, stupid, not my shoelaces.

[I fall on my nose. But that's alright. It's taken far more punishment in the ring]

LUSHOUS LOUISE   [marching out, heels detonating on the wooden floor] So long, suckers, see you in…

The Select Bar

BARNEY   [throwing down my second Double Diamond] I think that when you're hanging upside down people should pay more attention to you.

A VOICE   Higgins, you're just a show-off, says

HARRIET HIGGINS   [plonking herself down onto the lap of a small baldy man sat on his own] You don't mind me sitting here, do you darling?
   [she asks, delicately hitching her frock as she crosses her legs]

SMALL BALDY MAN   [recovering his composure] How d'you do.

HARRIET [taking out a powder compact, refreshing her ugly face[I'm alright, as far as a neglected wife can be'

UNCLE CECIL [previously banned from the Select invites himself in with a wooden mallet] I was a good little misogynist till I met the Blonde.

BARNEY Put the blame on anyone but yourself.

UNCLE CECIL Do not entreat the Mercy of St Agnes for none shall be given.

BARNEY The old fool, he's fallen for the Blonde's patter again.

THE BLONDE [aka St Agnes, enters much to the chagrin of Lushous Louise] Come along, Barney, I'll let you buy me a new corset.

  [She turns, crooks her little finger, walks slowly away, pulling me behind her with the aid of my penis]

THE BLONDE Uncle Cesspit do your duty.

  [There are cries and shouts as Uncle Cecil runs round the bar clouting the clientele with his wooden mallet]

THE BLONDE   Don't feel sorry for Harriet.

BARNEY   I don't.

THE BLONDE   She has no trouble finding punters who prefer....

BARNEY   The grog-blossomed blowzy type.

THE BLONDE   You have her down to a tee. Are you susceptible yourself?

BARNEY   Only when she flaunts her big arse and even then only if she's wearing nylons and suspenders.

THE BLONDE   You show a fine sense of discrimination. No floozie is going to seduce you.

Only high-class ones like you shouts

UNCLE CECIL   [as he runs by us into the street] Jesus Christ, the things you make me do.

BARNEY   I didn't know he has religious feelings.

THE BLONDE   I find him useful though strictly speaking he shouldn't be let out without a male nurse.

   [We stand back as lightning flashes and lo, the heavens open up on Uncle Cecil and we see a great rain descending in a torrent and falling upon him.
   Here comes a blooded beauty]

LUSHOUS LOUISE   Where's that bastard, Uncle Cecil?   Oh look who it is. I hope he's more use to you than he was to me last night.

THE BLONDE   I can make mountains out of molehills.

BARNEY   Course you can.

   [I hope. Best not to dwell on last night. That wasn't the shag that was. It's over, let it be.
   It's still raining. We go back in]

BARNEY   Leave that woman alone, she's bad enough with her nerves as it is
   [I say to the Crusher, who is strangling the wife]

THE CRUSHER   She called me the Milky Bar Kid.

THE BLONDE   What do you expect, decked out in those chaps and boots.

THE CRUSHER   I was going line dancing.

BARNEY   He has the mentality for it   [aside] Never grew up proper. His old ma still has to half-chew his grub for him.

THE BLONDE   Mouth to mouth?

BARNEY   Best not to think about it.

HARRIET   [crawling over] Another bimbo to take out in your Jaguar? How many does it hold?

BARNEY   She's just jealous cos I don't take her out in it.

THE BLONDE   Envy is so unbecoming.

BARNEY   I can't have a social lie without her nagging and running to priests.

THE BLONDE   I don't know how you stand it.

BARNEY   Well you have to these days, don't you, but yes it does take its toll. It's a proven fact that the biggest cause of high blood pressure in men is wives.

   [In comes a breathless runner]

SLEEPY SID   Barney! Barney! the Bogies have just lifted Mrs O'Harnessey and are holding her for ransom. She's in the Cannon Street nick.

BARNEY   They wouldn't dare.

HARRIET   Yes they would now that I persuaded Antichrist Atlas to strip her of her charisma.

THE BLONDE   Now we can see her as she really is.

BARNEY   Don't be too nonchalant. I do believe that Harriet is out to deprive me of all my girlfriends and you could be next.

THE BLONDE   I never thought of that.

BARNEY It don't bear thinking about'

SLEEPY SID You better do something about Mrs O. It's more than your life's worth if you don't.

BARNEY I'm broke.

THE BLONDE Don't look at me.

BARNEY I know. Those stiffs Harriet keeps down in the cellar courtesy of Uncle Cecil.

SLEEPY SID He's a right menace with that mallet so he is.

THE BLONDE I do try to control him but….

BARNEY It's warm down here. Who's the guvnor?

CHIEF STIFF I am. She calls me Mr Pastry.

BARNEY Good news. You're all free to go.

MR PASTRY   Not so fast. If we go out you won't let us back in. We've been committed to this here asylum and there aint nothing you can do about it.

BARNEY   You're wasting away down here when you could be worth something.

MR PASTRY   Like what? We've got loads of grub, plenty of sugars in our char and are not made to have baths.

BARNEY   If you put your mind to it you could all be hostages.

MR PASTRY   Hostages? Are they valuable?

BARNEY   They certainly are.

MR PASTRY   That's alright then. It's nice to be valuable.

BARNEY   [to Harriet who is crawling in] This lot aren't up to hostage standard. There's not a brain cell between them.

HARRIET   I dint mean to turn them into zombies. I just wanted docile pets who love me.

BARNEY   Now we'll never get Mrs O out of nick.

HARRIET   We can sell them to WooWang to play Russian Roulette with.

BARNEY   Or to the Government labs to test new drugs to put in the water.

HARRIET   I think they're already using loonies for that….Oh Barney, I hope they didn't experiment on you when you was sectioned.

BARNEY   Your concern is touching, seeing how you and Dr Ragamuffin signed me in.

HARRIET   What was it like?

BARNEY   I heard bells ringing and had a terrible vision.

HARRIET   Are you able to talk about it?

BARNEY   It was Uncle Cecil in his nightshirt running through the town like a moonstruck Wee Willie Winkie.

HARRIET   Oh Barney, no mortal should be exposed to such horror – not even you. How you stood it I don't know. How can I make it up to you?

BARNEY   It all comes down to nylons with a seam.

HARRIET   No, you're not getting into my knickers, not until you get rid of your tarts.

BARNEY   Think of your marriage vows.

  [I've always said hypocrisy has its uses]

MR PASTRY   Lady Harriet, most beloved, we are proud to offer you this tribute.

  [He kneels and hands her a tin of used cigarette butts, and the Lady Harriet in gratitude leads him down the passage and locks him up in her isolation wardrobe.
  I've done time in that Lubyanka era wardrobe when it belonged to Mrs Grantly-Hogg as did a Jehovah Witness who knocked upon her door.
  Let us go over like Asmodeus to see what's happening in....

Alimonia

Amelia Grantly-Hogg's pinched face comes into view and look there's Uncle Cecil dressed as a monk, his wet clothes neatly hung up, and he's holding Amelia's holy-water sprinkler (a club set with spikes)

AMELIA   You're not far off the medieval mark.

   [Looking on are her three husbands, holding up their trousers, their belts confiscated for giving surly looks.
   Uncle Cecil dances over and threatens them with his sprinkler.
   Amelia, that highly-strung horsewoman, just out of the Shires, strides over in her tight black jodhpurs]

AMELIA   Am I not one of the top equestriennes in England?
   [The gagged husbands can only nod vigorously due to Amelia's reasonable desire for them to be seen and not heard] Only flesh and blood can stand it
   [she says, her blue-tipped fingers exploring the stigmata that resulted from their devious attempts to escape by falling down the stairs. She regards Uncle Cecil, points to the floor]
Comme ci, comme ca.

[He lies down. She puts one foot on the shaft of his penis]

UNCLE CECIL   How well you place yourself, Missus, I can only imagine how much practice was involved.

AMELIA   Yers, it's a top technique.

[and as she stands on him, shifting her weight, she induces a forceful ejaculation]

The Panhandle

That's enough of that. Like Sir Patrick Spens I'm walking on the Strand. I met Billie just out of Holloway. She's my last chance. I'm broke and out of smokes. The Blonde, Eddie and Lushous Louise have stopped being my girlfriends and are making me pay for it. That's what I call a cartel.

BARNEY   [singing]   As I'm walking along the Strand with Billie   and the band begins to play
oh, Billie, Billie, Billie
it don't matter what they say.

15

BILLIE   I'd like to go to the Hot Sheets Hotel with you but I've got to meet my probation officer.

BARNEY   I'll take you there. His office is at the Cannon Street nick.

Quean Anne's Footstool

MRS O'HARNESSEY   You did well, Higgins. A prisoner exchange was an inspired idea.

BARNEY   How I think them up I don't know.

MRS O'HARNESSEY   Yes you may be mad but you're not stupid.

BARNEY   What happened to my copy of the *Beano*?

MRS O'HARNESSEY   I can't bide people who read in the lav.

BARNEY   Catch me doing that.

MRS O'HARNESSEY   I have done.

   [She puts her hand under the pillow case covering my head, strokes my cheeks, making noises with the bristles, slaps my face, I take hold of her hand, kiss it, a backhander sets my shop teeth rattling. And they say romance is dead.
   Mrs O doesn't have to be nice to me. She appeals direct to Widmerpool (my penis) and cuts out the middle man]

BARNEY   Can't I take this thing off now?

THE ANTICHRIST   Not long now. I'm giving her a new improved charisma and you will be amazed.

At home

Aunty Atlas the arch-fiend of Scotland has elevated Harriet to the rank of

LADY BROOMHILDA   Barney get up and answer the door.

[Enter the Squire with a leek behind his ear]

BARNEY   Here's another head the ball.

THE SQUIRE   Ah Lady Broomhilda, come with me to Emma's Farm, let me chase you through the ponds and heaps of hay of your heart's desire and there in one final act of exhortation you may make my cock crow.

LADY BROOMHILDA   Such language as I never hoped to hear.

THE SQUIRE   Can I help it if my heart is pierced by Lady Broomhilda's arrow?

BARNEY   [to Harriet]   There's been goings on here, I just know it.

LADY BROOMHILDA   Spoken like a true peasant.

BARNEY   A man can take it and take it then there comes a time when he can take it no more.

[I get up, put on my hat]

LADY BROOMHILDA   Barney, Barney, please don't go.

[But I'm adamant. I brush aside her clinging hand, open the door. It's pouring down. I go back to my armchair by the fire. I say to her

BARNEY   You're on a warning.

[I take out a little black book from my jacket. I write down her name]

Dockland

I've been made Special Agent by Major Peppar and I have the badge to prove it.
   I creep up the stairs. Her door is open. That makes me think but not enough. There's an aura of perfume and stockinged thighs.
   A small voice says
   Watch yourself.
   But I'm not listening.
   There's a table with books on it. I put my finger against the spine of *The Man from Laramie*, crouch down…

BARNEY [whispering] This is it, bub, spill your guts or fade.

A VOICE [making me jump] That's telling him.

[It's Miss Stark with a hard face and a pistol pointed at where I keep my ulcers.
 I make a great spring for the door and I would have made it too if my bad back hadn't given out, making me stumble and stagger bent over till I trip on the shaggy rug by the door and fall awkwardly with the handle nearly taking my ear off]

BARNEY You'll pay for this
 [I warn her, getting to my feet.
 I feel a spasm of deep regret as I lift my hat, push back the spectacles on my bloody ear and walk out]

Auntie Atlas summons me to the annual Ceremony of the Well.
 At the bottom lives a critter which only Auntie can control.

BARNEY [in a dog's collar, throwing down lumps of bread and cups of tea] And one by one they drop some more onto the varmint's harvest floor.

[But all is not as planned. Slouching towards me, his black stick beating a sinister rhythm on the ground is

BERNARD HOLLAND   Leave that critter alone.

[Here they come in their suits, hats and sunglasses, the Tonton Macoutes of Bernard Holland's master, Papa Doc. They fire stun guns at me. I'm bound hand and foot to a cross. I hang there on a hill. I am humble but not meek]

HARRIET   [crawling towards me] Barney Higgins, you get down from that cross. You know you've been excommunicated.

[Auntie Atlas pushes her out of the way. She grabs my cojones and laughs in my face as she conjures up a storm.
   Next thing she's riding in a chariot, her long hair flying in the air like Boudicca.
   Then she's behind me, whispering in my ear]

AUNTIE ATLAS   You have one chance only to avoid being the next critter in the well. Will you take it?

BARNEY   Yes, yes, I'll do anything.

AUNTIE ATLAS   Even the Barrel of Repentance?

[The Barrel of Repentance!]

BARNEY   Yes, even that.

AUNTIE ATLAS   Very well.

CHORUS   Roll out the barrel

[I'm in it alright but I can push my arms through the holes in the sides so I'm not entirely helpless.
   Harriet is reading out from *The Mammoth Book of Wives' Grievances*]

Enter INSPECTOR GORSE   Higgins, you have knobbly knees, you know that don't you?

HARRIET   [consulting the index] Ah yes, page 387.

INSPECTOR GORSE   Ever been to the Isle of Wight?

Parkhurst

WARDER   You've got a visitor. It's Miss Jane again.

   [Who?
   You never saw eyes so blue.
   No, not her from Shoreditch or her of the fighting ships or her used to be in the *Daily Mirror*.
   This Jane is a very clever frail who visits me in jail. She thinks it's an exciting place to be where she can rub up against manly types like me who shower only once a week]

JANE   [slowly pulling off her gloves] Oh Barney, let me be your dame savant. Look at my nails. See how they flaunt.

BARNEY   How'd you know about me and nails?

JANE   The parole board knows all about you. They de-brief Cousin Betsey once a month.

BARNEY   Cousin Betsey?

JANE Yes Barney, butter does melt in her mouth.

WARDER Time's up.

JANE Don't fret, my love. I'll wait for you. I'll wait for you in Kalamazoo. [Exits]

[Well I'll be gormed. It's Lovely Miss Nightingale come to tell me I'm not alone. She's Major Peppar's lovely controller. I expect I'm undercover again like the spy who came in from the cold.
This is an odd case when you come to think of it. Which I try not to do.

I'm on the loose again,
Lovely Miss Nightingale has told me to follow Cousin Betsey. She's appearing at the Empire in Leicester Square.

COUSIN BETSEY The dame makes a curtsey, the dog makes a bow, the dame says Your servant, the dog says Bow Wow.

[How provocative she is. That Bow Wow is too much for the rabble. They roar and stamp and try to storm the stage. A shot rings out]

A DAME   So they haf found me. I should haf known I could not escape from them.
   [she sits down, crosses her legs. Those shapely nyloned thighs with their fully fashioned stockings don't sidetrack me one bit]
Fate has brought you here. Only you can stop the secrets leaving the country. You must go to Scotland. But hurry, it is a matter of days, perhaps hours.

   [I haven't a clue who this Judy is but I have a foreboding. Let her out of your sight and she'll be staggering around with a knife in her back before you can say Jack Robinson.
   I better get out of here before they pin it on me]

Back in the Panhandle

Clothilda, the fattest woman to ever sail round the world, is strangling me with my own tie.
   I'm not terribly fussed as Harriet often throttles me as I'm sleeping so I'm quite immune.

CLOTHILDA Hey you! Get over here.

[Razor Ramsay the Second jumps up, the bubble gum he was blowing bursts onto his ugly mug]

Higgins says he was only at the theatre to watch *Puss in Boots*.

RAZOR RAMSAY THE SECOND I don't like coincidences. Let me finish him off.

CLOTHILDA Too dangerous. Besides, if he knew anything he'd have told us by now.

RAZOR RAMSAY THE SECOND You may be right. He may be a clapped-out private eye but he don't like cops and he don't drop dimes.

[Actually I do now and again. But only for the purpose of revenge or personal gain]

CLOTHILDA Okay Higgins you can go but remember if you know anything keep it zipped.

RAZOR RAMSAY THE SECOND Or else.

[I get out of the chair, lift my hat and walk out. It's teeming down.

I put my collar up, pull down the brim of my hat and the rain runs down into my mouth]

The Badlands

A VOICE   Peppar's the name and treason's the game.

O'ROURKE   It's proud I am [says the carrot-topped bruiser] to be of service to a true patriot such as yourself.

MAJOR PEPPAR   Not quite right. I'm more of a traitor if you follow me….I'll teach 'em to accuse me of borrowing mess funds.

O'ROURKE   Ach, a fine gentleman such as yourself always has creditors at his heels.

BARNEY   I'm tortured by them too.

MAJOR PEPPAR   Well, we're in the right place, Navigator-General, to gather up your navvies.

O'ROURKE   Aye, it seems only yesterday dat the Hill-Bills came down from those hills, ravaging and taking prisoners

BARNEY   Them were the days.

O'ROURKE   They don't make Irish like dem no more.

MAJOR PEPPAR   Point of order, old chap, they were English.

O'ROURKE   How'd you know dat?

MAJOR PEPPAR   Tacitus in his chronicle makes it quite clear. They were carrying unbrellas.

O'ROURKE   They were not. 'Twas the pipes they were playing.

   [Shoves come to blows. The navvies gather round ominously]

MAJOR PEPPAR   Barney, help me out here.

   [I suppose I have to. He's paying me. And besides O'Rourke is far too guttural for my liking.
   Just then, Harriet rides up on her bike, throws me my mail-order

revolver.
  The navvies freeze when they see that.

O'ROURKE Go on lads, 'tis only a fake.

[I am as surprised as anyone when there's a bit of a roar and one of the navvies keels over holding his shoulder, and just for fun I shoot two more of them in the legs]

BARNEY Get out of it the lot of youse.
  [The navvies scurry off]
And you too, Major Peppar, I don't need company when I'm with a pretty girl.

  [I take Harriet in my arms and sing to her If you were the only girl in the world…]

Dockland

COUSIN BETSEY [opening the door] Oh Barney, you're chasing me again.

BARNEY   I've come about the parole board.

   [I hear a noise in the bedroom]

COUSIN BETSEY   It's only Sleepy Sid. He's just adjusting his dress before leaving.

   [He comes out. It's a blue one with spots]

SLEEPY SID   My advice to you is don't take your landlady for granted.

COUSIN BETSEY   I suppose Mrs O'Harnessey has thrown you out again….Barney, can't you take him in?

BARNEY   All my body-bags are full.

COUSIN BETSEY   Never mind, it was only a chimney.

SLEEPY SID   Better than being homeless.

   [Entre nous, the humpy wee bastard used to be a top alchemist mixing potions like spit and polish and elbow grease. He came out of a puzzle factory much worse than he went in]

BARNEY   Go back to the hedge you were born in.

SLEEPY SID   The Duke of Wellington said being in a stable doesn't make you a horse.

COUSIN BETSEY   You want to hear what Mrs O says about you, Barney.

BARNEY   She says I only exist in her imagination. I'd like to see her face if it turns out I'm a hologram.

COUSIN BETSEY   Don't you think Sleepy looks like a wizened elf?

SLEEPY SID   [singing and dancing round the room, holding his dress above his head] I'm not going out with Jane tonight, I'm not going out with Mary, I'm not going out with any girl, cos I'm a fairy.

Dockland

MAJOR PEPPAR   Make no mistake, this is a dangerous mission.

BARNEY   A Tinkerton knows his duty.

MAJOR PEPPAR   You need to catch Auntie Atlas when her powers are weakest.

BARNEY   When's that?

MAJOR PEPPAR   When she's on the toilet.

Let's not go into details. When you see me again I'm inside a giant clock and every quarter of an hour I'm propelled out and I shout
Cuckoo, cuckoo, cuckoo.
   And that's not all. Uncle Cecil's here with his holy water sprinkler. He's well into his Panglossian twilight but let's not forget that

UNCLE CECIL   Cracked pots often last longer.

  [And I thought being a weather vane was bad.
  As I come out he takes a swing at me and I hear

A VOICE   Don't be a bore in Baltimore.

[Yes, it's Lovely Miss Nightingale come to save me.
But it's not. It's Amelia Grantly-Hogg.

AMELIA   [keeping her two faces under one hood] And what do I see? A spy come to bring distempers down upon me.
   [she signals to her henchmen, Muldoon and Bucky Buchanan]
Take him away and biff him proper.

   [But she hasn't counted on the difference between a former pro boxer and two amateurs]

AMELIA   [kneeling before me] Dear Barney, show mercy to your dutiful controller.

UNCLE CECIL   What a load you have taken off my mind.

   [This is when I hit him]

AMELIA   Come now, Barney, how'd you like to be made foreman of the chain-gang at Alimonia? The sky's the limit.

[I hope you're reading between the lines here. it's not easy, I know, but this is a morality play about the disaffection from society of those we call outcasts.
  But it all depends on what you call Society, doesn't it?
  And whether you know it when you see it.
  I'm in danger of being philosophical here so I'll briefly mention how Amelia's stocking tops and suspenders contrast with the white skin of her thighs]

BARNEY [picking up Uncle Cecil and patting his head] Sorry about that, you're too ancient and simple.

UNCLE CECIL Ah'm awae back tae the British Museum be way o' Edenburrow.

  [see the way the old fool talks Scotch when he has a drop taken]

BARNEY I've taken a number of powders in my time but never with an hyperborean detour.

  [Don't get me wrong. He has his own way of returning to the British Museum, to which he was donated, and it's not for me to pass remarks on it.
  Or perhaps it is. I wouldn't go to Birmingham by way of Beachy Head and neither would you, so why he should take the risk of falling

into the hands of robbers and Scotch magistrates is beyond me.

Or maybe it isn't. Going up north should hold no fears for someone who was Hadrian's envoy to the Painted People.

So he tells me.

Watch him go, looking back and a-waving of his neckerchief as he strolls down the lane into his future.

And we have to give him his dues. Uncle Cecil is a much greater reprobate than people give him credit for]

PART TWO

Office of a shyster lawyer.

When you think of Fat Patricia you think of Mrs Thompson's dowdy brothel down at the Markets.

Well, don't you?

She's dowdy too. Fat Patricia. £ signs in her eyes but money can't buy taste nor moderate her broad Ulster accent.

FAT PATRICIA   [growing dishonestly old with a straight face] Put away your brass rubbings. I've taken an abnormal attachment to you.

[She's talking to Michael Meddler. He's as greedy as she is. How else could he have paid big money for his nose hairs to be transplanted on his blind alley of a dome]

MICHAEL MEDDLER   You said no strings attached.

FAT PATRICIA   I said nothing about chains.

NAMELESS HUSBAND   I've, er, a good mind to---

FAT PATRICIA   [holding his nose to the grindstone] Get back to work, you runt.

Enter MRS O'HARNESSEY   Forgive my girlish sniggering but you don't have to be so literal.

FAT PATRICIA   [buttoning up her coat over her bloomers] I'm a country gab and proud of it.

MRS O'HARNESSEY   Gabardine is so yesterday.

Enter AUNTIE ATLAS   Forasmuch as it pleases the Great Panjandrum of his great mercy to take unto hisself the goods of our dear sister soon to be departed, we therefore commend her pot-belly to the depths of Hell, already turned into corruption, looking for the resurrection of her husband's organ when the sea shall give up its dead.

CHORUS   O hear us when we cry to thee, for those in peril on the sea.

>[A curtain falls.
>Enter a well-dressed man in a suit, snap-brim hat and a green bow-tie]

BARNEY   Au nom du people authentique justice est faite.

The Footstool

Mrs O'Harnessey in her pranks gave poor Alfred forty wanks, when she saw what she had done she told him it was all in fun.

Alfred goes off to change his prostate, past the angular spinsters of little future and here comes

MRS UPPER CRUST [curling one's lip and feeling frightfully irritable] I say, though thou exalt yourself as Mrs O'Harnessey and set your saddle among the stars, thence will I bring thee down, saith the Lone Ranger.

MRS O'HARNESSEY   We schoolmistresses must keep terrible order you know.

MRS UPPER CRUST   You are one of those too?

MRS O'HARNESSEY   Yes I used to be a hairdresser as well, until the day Teasy Weasy stole my scissors. I never got over it and to maintain my peace of mind I became an apologist for perpetual punishment.

MRS UPPER CRUST   A cri de coeur, if I ever heard one.

MRS O'HARNESSEY   I didn't want to fight but by jingo I did. I had the whips, the poison pens and a slave called Sleepy Sid.

MRS UPPER CRUST   I expect one can suck up quite a bit of venom into a Parker.

MRS O'HARNESSEY   Yes but do it with panache.

MRS UPPER CRUST   Back in the old regime when Lady Muck and I dined with Pappy Doc we used up all the partridges he shot---

MRS O'HARNESSEY   Perdrix, toujours perdrix.

MRS UPPER CRUST   Quite. We had a page-boy called Parker who was tasked with looking after the snakes. Pappy gave him venom injections to build up his immunity in case he was bitten.

MRS O'HARNESSEY   He was so kind-hearted.

MRS UPPER CRUST   Known for it. And he let me do it. Once a day in his cheeks. But he over-reacted. Before long he had a head like a Mekon.

MRS O'HARNESSEY   Typical male. I've seen them swell up at the slightest instigation. My latest example of which is called....
   [Flourish of trumpets]
....Barney Higgins, caught in flaggers with one of my charladies. Sixty five if she's a day.

MRS UPPER CRUST   Wouldn't have happened on my estate. Sir Gerald wouldn't even look at a menial over fifty. We had a second staircase built so he wouldn't meet them on the stairs.

Enter BARNEY   If you ask me it's a question of ageism.

MRS O'HARNESSEY   Hark at him. We don't need lessons from a former bricklayer like you.

BARNEY   [suddenly contrite]   Yes I did brick Harriet up in the cellar and she's never let me forget it.

Enter HARRIET   I wouldn't have minded so much but it was on our honeymoon.

BARNEY   I was only putting you in purdah. So full of eastern promise you were and you still have that schoolgirl complexion.

CHORUS   You'll be a little lovelier each day with fabulous pink Camay.

MRS UPPER CRUST   Yes Lady Broomhilda, what is your secret?

HARRIET   Well since you ask, I use a face-mask of maggots.

BARNEY   Top breeders recommend it.

HARRIET   They eat the hard skin, you see.

MRS UPPER CRUST   You have such weird knowledge.

HARRIET   Yes, when Barney calls me a witch I take it as a compliment.

   [Don't look now but there's an apparition creeping up]

AUNTIE ATLAS   Has anyone seen my book of spells?

   [It was me but I'm saying nothing. I was just looking at it, frowning, trying to puzzle out what it meant.
   It burst into flames.
   Couldn't take it, see. Direct exposure to the mind of a deranged detective.
   The priest himself got hot when I told him to stop making mysteries out of molehills.
   Back thunders

THE VATICAN   You watch it, Barney Higgins, or you'll get it across the back of the legs.

BARNEY   Get lost. I'm not in one of your orphanages anymore.

Here's a new face for you

TOMMY TIPTOE   Ah'm as crabbed as thae come, country dishes leave me cold but ma strange heart goes pit a pat for a city lass known as

MISS FROSTY PANTS   I am a scowling secret lovelady who arouses clumpish devotion. I give men nary a glance as I ride proudly past on

FRANCIS THE TALKING MULE   She's a frivolous tart. I mean, what good is a straw hat and a necklace made of treacle when you need four new shoes? Answer me that.

BARNEY   Give over. There's plenty would like to be in your position.

   [Oh, here's another new face. He didn't like the old one]

HERMAN   Call me Hermanicus. And I have the stigmata to prove it.

   [Would you believe it. I nail the wretch to Eddie's cross and he's all proud of it]

MISS FROSTY PANTS   I know that face! It looks in my windows.

BARNEY   Sorry, Herman, I'm sending you back to Santy's Grotto.

TOMMY TIPTOE   Ah've a sofa he can rent. Wouldnae cost much.

BARNEY   [to Herman] Don't go there. You can see the herpes jumping off the cushions.

   [The next time I see his face it's not at a window. It's looking at me from the T.V. screen and it's not even turned on.

HERMAN   It is, you know. Auntie tuned it into the ether world.

Sitting with her legs crossed in a warm corner of a small kitchen somewhere over the M62, Ester the chemist from Cologne casts a weary eye over the bossbacked and bandy-legged figure of Sleepy Sid whom she is training to be a garden gnome.

ESTER   [to O'Rourke, Navigator-General, who is sniffing round her] Vat 'ave sie found out?

O'ROURKE   The New Gestapo has put out an APB on Barney Higgins.

[That's me. I'm inside a statue of Tonto. I was hoping for an upgrade to the Lone Ranger but there's time for that yet]

ESTER   They shall not 'ave him.

O'ROURKE   Why not? You're all Krauts together aint you?

ESTER   Ja wohl! But the Great Panjandrum does not them trust.

O'ROURKE   Is that because---

ESTER   Ja, too much he knows.

[Sound of high heels approaching. I like to think of them making dents in the lino.
  Sound of knocking]

ESTER   Capitain Moonlight, are you there?

BARNEY   I could take a cup of tea.

ESTER   O'Rourke vill set you free. Put Germany first und you vill never regret it.

O'ROURKE [singing] For they're hangin' men and women for the wearing of the green…

[I'm a Paddy myself but I don't give my allegiance to foreign institutions. There's enough English doing that.
And once again we hear the mighty roar of an aggrieved Harriet. She's got her warpaint on and I get a glimpse of an umbrella as she rushes into the room]

HARRIET Come out, Higgins, wherever you are.

[Ester screams and O'Rourke takes to his heels as the bayonet at the end of her brollie flashes past their noses]

Collars and cuffs.

And lo, the black angel comes upon them and beats all round her and they are sore afraid.

[We're at Eddies place where she does the tailoring]

MADAME MAO [guest dominatrix] Put your belly on the floor, you fat lump
   [she commands the Crusher, sitting on his back pulling back his ears]

HARRIET   Leave him alone. He called me Baby Doll a year ago.

MADAME MAO   But he likes it, n'est-ce-pas?

   [As usual Harriet gets the wrong end of the stick unlike Portuguese Joe whom Eddie has over a chair. I make an excuse and leave]

It's the next day at the Footstool.

MRS O'HARNESSEY   You're a fool to yourself, Barney Higgins, taking up with that Madame Mao. It's terrible the way she exploits people.

BARNEY   What's this all about?

MRS O'HARNESSEY   It's about the Garden of Oblivion. [a rival organization] We need a hermit of our own.

BARNEY   Didn't know they kept hermits.

MRS O'HARNESSEY   They don't. That's the point. Try to keep up.

   [I'm not sure she's being quite fair. But the ways and means of the Footstool are incomprensible to me. I suspect she makes them up as she goes along]

MRS O'HARNESSEY   [her mouth twisting in an ugly smile] I heard that. Try not to move your lips when you think. I am always fair and to prove it I will give you a full sixty minutes to find me a hermit, which will put one over on the Garden of Oblivion.

   [Here comes Harriet, full as a fool, leading the Crusher down the garden path, the pair of them singing, She loves me, yea, yea.
   I look questionably at Mrs O]

MRS OHARNESSEY   [shaking her head] I am grooming her as a nun and when I tell her to renounce the world you as a bricklayer will have the honour of sealing her inside her cell. That'll be another poke in the eye for that Garden of Oblivion.

BARNEY   Foreman bricklayer if you don't mind.

MRS O'HARNESSEY   Why's Crusher dressed as a soldier?

BARNEY   Don't ask, but Guardsmen do it.

MRS O'HARNESSEY   It don't bear thinking about.

BARNEY   Not even for experienced landladies.

[She goes over to the Crusher,, clouts him several times on the chops]

THE CRUSHER   [stuttering]   What's that for?

MRS O'HARNESSEY   You know.

[All this dreaming of army camps has done him no good. He once joined the Household Cavalry and spent a year peeling vegetables]

My office

Eddie's not as stupid as she looks. She keeps her brains hidden behind a low neckline.

BARNEY   [singing] Oh Eddie, you have tossed and turned, and for Barney you have yearned, so come with me this very day, over the hills and far away.

EDDIE   Kiss me Barney, Barney, kiss me.

  [She's not well, you know. Been under the doctor for weeks. Never mind what for. Even Eddie deserves some privacy.
  She falls to the floor. I reach for her smelling salts]

A VOICE   Hey you! Leave that girl alone.

  [It's Bert. Her boyfriend till he went into Parkhurst]

BARNEY   I don't think we've met
  [I say, feinting with a handshake and hooking with my left. He lands on Eddie. She starts shouting]

CHORUS Bert, Bert, the piper's son, learned to play when he was young, but the only tune that he could play was Over the hills and far away.

The Fishmongers Hall

Every three months adherents of the Footstool gather to record the lucre they have obtained by stealing and prostitution for the one known as

THE MATRON [aka Mrs O'Harnessey] you may consider yourselves the forty thieves but it is Matron, your large as love liege-ladiy, who has liens on all your life assurances and can at any time lift her heel against your bony necks.
   Lip service will get you nowhere because I am out for what I can get. And when I recall the martyrs of this Footstool I recall in effect the martyrs of this Footstool

   [The Squire is not the only one who talks nonsense]

Yes [she continues] the pirates who fell in the Ditch, cruelly put down in their light-fingered prime.
   And now you await with eager hearts the name of the top provider

of the last quarter.
And the answer is
  [Roll of drums]
Roger of the Hill!

   [He steps up, emotions unseen in the vacuum of his unmade face. His prize is unlimited gusset-stroking in the company of Elsie the Suicide Blonde.
   The assembly breaks into a chorus of the

MATRON SONG   A fairer matron there never was seen
than Mrs O'Harnessey the Footstool's queen.
There's wild coyotes and strawberries too,
and she won't wash dishes nor mop out the loo.

MATRON   And now for the blunderhead who came last...
PIANO MUSIC   Roll out the barrel

   [There's great merriment in the crowd. Matron looks through slitted eyes at the unhouseled creatures pushing each other in crude saltation, frenzied by Portuguese Joe's honktonk pianner]

MATRON   An the one who came last was....

[It's no surprise to see Harriet being wheeled out in the Barrel of Repentance]

HARRIET   It's so unfair! I can't be a nun and walk the streets too.

MATRON   You can multi-task, can't you? There's a market for that type of thing,

[I'd like to help her but there's not much I can do considering I'm bound in packing tape, lying as a Trojan horse at Matron's feet.
 The idea is that I roll down into the first row where Calypso's couriers are sitting in disguise.
 They'll take me back to the Garden of Oblivion, Calypso's underground den which she hasn't left in twenty years because she's an albino.
 Yes, it's an absurd and dangerous undercover mission but Captain Moonlight is his own hero.
 He has to be because most people think he's useless]

HARRIET   [calling] Barney Higgins, come you back here, come you back here.

Back at the Footstool

MRS O'HARNESSEY   Sit there and be quiet.
  [I'm on the Stool of Shame. Those men I thought were Calypso's couriers were federal agents investigating Matron's mailfraud]
You're lucky I got Fat Patricia to take the rap.

BARNEY   She always was greedy.

MRS O'HARNESSEY   Now what am I to do with Portuguese Joe? Has he the makings of a hermit?

BARNEY   You have one already. You shouldn't put two hermits in together.

MRS O'HARNESSEY   The Crusher's no good. He has no odour of sanctity. And he keeps escaping when he hears the chimes of an icecream van.

BARNEY   Don't they have any other tune but Greensleeves.

MRS O'HARNESSEY   Good point, Barney, but not strictly relevant.

BARNEY   What will this new hermit do all day?

MRS O'HARNESSEY   Contemplate on me of course. And - I have just decided on a whim – he shall wear an iron mask.

BARNEY   Be careful, Matron, these men in the iron masks are always causing trouble.

MRS O'HARNESSEY   Not if they're shackled.

BARNEY   That's one way to stop them running after icecream vans.

Later

A hooter sounds.

BARNEY   Time for chow.

[Ester the chemist from Cologne enters pushing a trough on wheels. Her Russian POW's hurry over on their knees. They are dismayed to see what's in it. Nothing. German humour.

ESTER   [to Mrs O] Such an excellent joke, is it not?   [exits]

PORTUGUESE JOE   [serving time as a Russian POW] She has us in stitches
  [he says, holding out his bandaged arm then looking up as Harriet enters affecting the Grecian Bend with the aid of a big stone round her neck]

BARNEY   Whatever are you at?

HARRIET   I had an illumination on the way to Dame Ascot

BARNEY   Who's she?

HARRIET   She said I have to marry Jesus.

BARNEY   What's the stone for?

HARRIET   Jesus was stoned, wasn't he.

MRS O'HARNESSEY   Look here, my girl, don't you go listening to no Dame Ascots putting stuff into your head. Jesus was crucified, see.

[He could have been stoned too but you don't say that when Mrs O is in her Mother Superior frame of mind]

Miss Wink's Academy

Formerly Barney's Home for Unwanted Wives.

THE REV BROCKLEHURST [*pace* Jane Eyre. In his pyjamas and with a mortarboard on his head] My visit here is purely professional with a special vocation to the lost lovelies of London. [Whispering to Tommy Tiptoe] I hope you don't think I was trying to get off with them girls.

TOMMY TIPTOE Ma heed's in a spin already. Ah've given up on Frosty Pants.

UNCLE CECIL [the worse for wear] I'm just nicely thank you.

TOMMY TIPTOE It's dear here. D'ye think they give oot Green Shield stamps?

THE REV BROCKLEHURST I'll just take a wee peep in the Mirror of

Diana

[he says, going over to an old mirror on the wall that has seen much cellulite (and the occasional varicose vein) and he is rewarded by a vision of the Conductress, cig in mouth, cane swishing at her side, herding along the great lump of Portuguese Joe, a mooing Harriet and a chittering Herman on all fours.

But that's just him. The real Conductress is biding her time until the big moment when she ascends the specially constructed steps with her short skirt caught artfully in her panties]

TOMMY TIPTOE   [eyeing up Lushous Louise] Aye, ilka Jeanie has her Jockie and ah'm hers.

[He goes over, gives her a hug and gets a knee in his Henry Halls]

LUSHOUS LOUISE   Hugs by prior appointment only.

[She bends over, places her hands protectively over her wired bra and makes a moue at

BARNEY   I'll look after him
[I tell her and bounce Tommy Tiptoe down to the Catacombs below where I come across the Witch of Wookey.

And what, might you ask, is a mere hug to Lushous Louise?

Plenty. She may have a history of bra and panties with hand relief but she's moved on and is now the latest version of Miss Wink]

THE WITCH OF WOOKEY   [fading in and out] I'm here, Barney, I'm here! Look at my poor gnarled hands and withered nose. I'm in no-man's land, one foot in the ferry and a penny shoved in me gob.

BARNEY   Sounds sore.

THE WITCH OF WOOKEY   Take me back and I'll make you real.

BARNEY   Complete with a soul?

THE WITCH OF WOOKEY   Yes, yes.

BARNEY   Not a second-hand one.

THE WITCH OF WOOKEY   No, no. I'll bring down an Irish mist upon you and you will chase the Devil in Dublin City.

BARNEY   What's Old Bendy got to do with it?

THE WITCH OF WOOKEY   Come now, be reasonable. You need to get one that'll fit.

BARNEY   I'm not sure about this. Compromise myself with Old Bendy and it'll be all round the spirit world the next day.

THE REV BROCKLEHURST   [who mislaid his faith down the back of a sofa in Eddie's massage parlour] I may only be a rescuer of maidens but I could tell you a thing or two about witches.

[pause]

BARNEY   Well why don't you?

THE REV BROCKLEHURST   I was arrested in my pyjamas by Antichrist Atlas. You have the face of a disreputable milliner, she told me, and apart from supervised outings to the local Yates Wine Lodge I was imprisoned in a bandbox until she stopped menstruating.

  [A likely story. There are no Yates Wine Lodges in London. I hear a trumpet calling me]

BARNEY   Attention please. Pray be silent for the Chant of the Conductress.

THE DRIVERS   [chanting] Plain Jane is my Conductress, I shall not deny,
She maketh me to lie down on old tramlines.
She leadeth me by my penis to her Valley of Joy,
She restoreth my hard-on with the rub of her feet.
Yea, though I walk through sinks and stews and terminuses,
I shall dwell in the grip of the Conductress for ever.

[A roll of drums
   Plain Jane walks slowly and suggestively up the steps. At the top she says to an awed and entranced audience

note

PLAIN JANE   Take not all you homely and mousy women out there. Find out what excites men, dress accordingly, be provocative, and you shall never be without a date on Saturday night.

The Stranglers Arms

Harriet's away at a hag party with her old ma, Daisy
Dumpling, getting advice on how to sue me for desertion.
   (if you're in the house you are under their feet, if you keep out of

the way you're in the wrong too)

   I'm having a short one with a game publican called Clothilda, the fattest woman to ever sail round the world. Miss Adair, my well-stacked female secretary, is with me.

CLOTHILDA   You been in the Badlands before?

BARNEY   Been there? I used to terrorize the place.

MISS ADAIR   Him and the Lone Ranger.

BARNEY   Don't confuse me with the Cisco Kid.

CLOTHILDA   So you're not afraid of the Wikka Woman?

BARNEY   I say Bah to the old trout.

CLOTHILDA   You really got the sand for it, to take her out?

BARNEY   I've dated worse.

CLOTHILDA   Alright, take down this message for her.

   [Miss Adair licks the stub of a pencil, looks up expectantly. Clothilda begins]

MISS ADAIR   Hold on, this is blunt.

CLOTHILDA   Try the sharp end.
   [She puts the message in an envelope, seals it with a sloppy red kiss]
At the heart of her cult is a fanatical coterie of Ancient Mariners.

BARNEY   Miss Adair has a way with sailors.

MISS ADAIR   I call them stooges.

CLOTHILDA   That's not all. She keeps Uncle Cecil in her small kitchen and slaps him silly.

BARNEY   Might improve his looks.

CLOTHILDA   [smiling, to Miss Adair] Barney's no oil painting neither.

BARNEY Look who's talking.
 [is my witty response.
 This is were a get clouted. With an Irish screwdriver. I'm lying on the floor listening to these two jades running me down]

MISS ADAIR He's as good a fallguy as ever fell over his own feet. [Laughs] Just joking. But we better be careful. Captain Moonlight is very merciless when he's annoyed or laughed at.

 [Yes I'm mad at Miss Adair. In fact, I'm mad at both of them. Or maybe I'm just mad]

MISS ADAIR I don't do this very often
 [she says through the jumper she's pulling over her head.
 I can't believe it. She's letting Clothilda have a good grope at her while they think I'm still out of it.
 Alright, I can believe it. I'm just keeping the pot simmering while we await the arrival of

THE REV BROCKLEHURST [peppery as a Welshman]
How can you do such a thing? How can you cause such pain in the heart of Jesus?

BARNEY It's all this watching telly on a Sunday. It's ruining Christianity.

THE REV BROCKLEHURST   Oh you are so right. I don't have a Devil's box in my vicarage but I urge all those who succumb to the lure of Rediffusion to put a sheet over it on the Sabbath.

CLOTHILDA   Give over, you old hypocrite.

MISS ADAIR   [already half undressed]   Come on, big boy, come and rescue me.

THE REV BROCKLEHURST   [whispering to Miss Adair] I'm really not that big. The doctor diagnosed Failure to Thrive when I was little....And I'm not really a hypocrite, you know. I'm only C of E and I don't suppose that counts as a religion.

The Badlands

MISS ADAIR   [at the main gate]   Pay attention, alien creatures, this here is Captain Moonlight, scourge of Dockland, nemesis of bitter schoolmistresses and eminent duellist extraordinaire.

BARNEY   [ironically to Miss Adair]   Steady on there, you missed out the part I played in running through Wat Tyler.

MISS ADAIR   Yes, and here's the sword!

[a sword suddenly appears in my hand. I make a few practice thrusts as she shouts

MISS ADAIR   Let us in to see your witch. Or suffer the wrath of Captain Moonlight.

GIMP SENTRY   You can't come in today. It's a bank holiday.

MISS ADAIR   Correct me if I'm wrong but I wasn't aware that this is a bank.

GIMP SENTRY   Could be for all you know.

[Miss Adair walks up to him, pokes him in the chest and is not fazed by how far her finger goes in]

MISS ADAIR   Listen here, George---

GIMP SENTRY   Don't call me that. My name's Percy.

MISS ADAIR   What's wrong with George? It's a perfectly good name.

There's been kings and saints named that. But it's not good enough for you, oh no, you prefer a puffy name like *Percy*.

PERCY   Go away, go away, Wikka Woman's not at home today.

   [Time I made myself felt]

BARNEY   What's those carts of headless beggars doing here then, if she's not at home.

PERCY   Mere refuse from the topping shed. I meant "not at home" in the refined sense of not receiving visitors. Too subtle I fear for the likes of you.

A VOICE   We have interlopers?

   [It's a frow being carried in a sedan chair]

BARNEY   The Wikka Woman I presume.

THE FROW   Heavens no, I'm Edith of Nancy Town, on my way to a photo opportunity in a dreary Dutch studio. [To Percy] The usual stuff.

PERCY   High jump for both?

THE FROW   Just him. After lots of horrible torture.

PERCY   Of course.

[I have this sword. It says Made in the people's republic of Korea. I fence my way into this tunnel. I hide in a railcar. It starts to move. It's being pulled along by men in rags. We come to a halt, the men move aside to reveal a figure with white hair, red lips and red eyes. She's wearing a short skirt slit up the side.

CALYPSO   Not too Susie Wongish?
   [she asks, striking a pose that does justice to her hourglass figure. Mind you, it's a very big hourglass]

BARNEY   Don't tell me you're the Wikka Woman.

CALYPSO   Alright I won't.
   [I give her the note]
This is in code, it tells me to execute the bearer of this missive.
   [She starts to laugh]
Who does she think she is, telling the Wikka Woman what to do.

[steps closer, taps me on the nose]
Higgins, I'm going to give you the opportunity to save yourself. Are you willing to take it?

BARNEY   I'm always ready to save myself.

CALYPSO   Live here in the Garden of Oblivion as my consort and find the freedom of eternal peace. Many have come before you.

BARNEY   I saw them on the carts outside,

CALYPSO   I do regret not being able to venture outside. That's why this underground railway is such a boon. They bring the pilgrims down to me, it's so convenient.

BARNEY   Using beggars as pit-ponies.

CALYPSO   I always suspected you were sentimental. You must realize that poverty has its duties as well as its rights.

BARNEY   I've nothing against eternal peace but I'd rather not enter it just at the moment. Maybe later. Thanks all the same.

The Hot Sheets Hotel

was a temporary home for the migrates until such time as their council houses were refurbished. Claim you are a Christian and a homosexual and you're taken by the hand. Guaranteed. I don't know how they kept from sniggering when they passed each other in the corridors.

CHORUS   Let's be merry, let's be gay.

   [Say what you like about Calypso but it's due to her generosity that I am able to speak to you now in an unsacrificed state. She accepted Miss Adair in my place.
   I humbly walk to the appointed room.
   I am expecting company.
Billie is icumen in,
llude sing Barney
knickerwet and soft white flesh
from bum down to her knee
sing sing Barney.

   Billie turns Darwin on his head, she makes monkeys out of men.
   Here's Billie now. I hear her knocking and she can come in]

BILLIE   I don't normally do this, you know.

BARNEY   Of course not but it doesn't make you a bad woman if you do.

[She makes a lengthy and sensuous display of taking off her black silken gloves, building up to a climax of long red nails]

Miss Wink's Academy (brothel) and Private Lunatic Asylum

Now for some real shagging.

HARRIET   [crawling in]   What a thing to say!

BARNEY   Sorry, I do forget myself at times.

HARRIET   This is a sorry place. I'm glad I'm not Miss Wink anymore, now that Jesus wants me for his rainbow.

TOMMY TIPTOE   [eyeing the talent]   They come as a boon ain a blessing tae men, the lushous, the lassies ain thae Panhandle hen.

LUSHOUS LOUISE   Not on your Nellie, you Scotch git.

TOMMY TIPTOE   Lushous Louise came tae town a-riding on a pony, she put her knickers on ma heed…

LUSHOUS LOUISE   You'll be so lucky

TOMMY TIPTOE   …and said she wouldnae phone me.

UNCLE CECIL   [the worse for wear] I'm just nicely, thank you.

BARNEY   [waxing poetic with the chemist from Cologne] my head thou dost with fire anoint and thy teutonic plates move mountains.

   [That's more like it, though I will admit to watching Billie refresh her face with a powder puff and compact. Sex goddesses come and go but

CHORUS   Little things mean a lot.

   [However that's not to distance myself from the skill shown by dimpled skaters as they burl round and round divulging their knickers.

Here's

DICKLESS TRACY   Enjoy yourselves, boys. Sorry I can't join in but I'm just back from Brussels.

PLAIN JANE   They never learn, they keep going over there and getting their pockets picked.
   Also, our guest chef Monsewer Mackerel reports that he had his ears boxed by Barney Higgins.

HARRIET   Who like most bouncers thinks he can clobber people whenever he feels like it.

PLAN JANE   Yes Barney, you should know better at your age.

BARNEY   No need to make a federal case out of it
   [I tell her and go off in a huff but I soon snap out of it when I come to the Showcase of Splendour with Mrs O displaying her thunderous thighs and at her feet in classical pose is the hermit in his iron mask]

MRS O'HARNESSEY   Shoo him away
   [she tells me pointing at her former hermit who is down on one knee pointing a broomstick at her]

THE CRUSHER   Its alright, it's not loaded.

[Look out, here's

MISS STARK   So you're the bouncer. Come with me.

[We go down to where she keeps her experiments to see if the surplus population can hibernate during the winter to solve the food crisis, and if that's not being philanthropic I don't know what is.

MISS STARK   This one here won't go into suspended animation.

[I'm not surprised to see that it's that troublemaker Mr Pastry who is lying on his back]

BARNEY   He should be grateful you take the time to experiment on him, that's what I say.

MISS STARK   Quite so, who else would have anything to do with them.

[She sits astride Mr Pastry, starts to throttle him]

BARNEY   You are adept at artificial respiration, I see.

MISS STARK   Have to be, in my line of work.

MR PATRY   [opening an eye]   Please missee don't send me back to Van Dieman's Land.

BARNEY   He's raving.

MISS STARK   He gets confused. I used to hire them out as pallbearers at Von Dietrich's Funeral Home. If travellers can do it so can I.

BARNEY   I agree. There should be equal opportunities for all in this green and pleasant land.

MR PASTRY   It's not the oul work I mind. It's better than driveways. It's standing for hours singing those wretched dirges.

BARNEY   It's a question of attitude, you should try and get into the spirit of things.

THE WITCH OF WOOKEY   [fading in and out]   Help me, Barney, help me. I'm in the washing machine in the corner.

   [I go over to it. I give it a kick. It takes a braver man than me to let a witch out of one of John Bloom's notorious machines when it's on a spin cycle.

Part 3

Alimonia

It's Plough Monday. Uncle Cecil is hovering above the garter with the autocrat of matrimonial torment.

AMELIA   You have to be told you're stupid otherwise you wouldn't know. Say thank you.

UNCLE CECIL   [who would at this point agree to anything] Thank thee sweet mysterie.

AMELIA   I want Fat Patricia brought here, I want her chained on her back so she can really be the slut she is. Afterwards, I want her put in a sack, dragged to the lake and thrown in.
   And to ease your conscience, just in case you have one, I have to tell you her dark deeds put even you and me in the shade.

[And where am I while this is going on? I'm in her wardrobe.

To be more specific I am in biblical bondage next to go in the sack.

I make a noise like blowing into a beer bottle or the call of an owl]

UNCLE CECIL   Hark! 'Tis the Ghost of Barney Higgins.

AMELIA   [cowering down] Stay away, spirit, you are too early, we haven't drowned him yet.
  [To Uncle Cecil]
That's Higgins all over. He always comes too soon.
  [That's a matter of opinion]

UNCLE CECIL   Oh this is dire, we must invoke the Mercy of St Agnes.

[Who is represented in antiquity as kneeling on a pile of faggots]

AMELIA   You'll do no such thing.
  [The phone rings, she puts on her telephone voice]
Haylow aim afraid yew must hev the roeing nember.
  [She slams down the phone, shouts at Uncle Cecil]
That was the bloody Blonde. Why'd you bring her into it.

[A booming voice resonates]

THE GHOST OF BARNEY HIGGINS   Ye have learnt nothing from Adam's original sins. Ye have joined with Harriet in tormenting the blameless and prayerful Barney Higgins.
   But mark ye this. He like Dreyfus will be vindicated at your displeasure and downfall.

MUSIC   The Marseillaise

UNCLE CECIL   Spare me, O spirit and I will take a revolver into a quiet room and be a gentleman to the end.

AMELIA   Rather defeats the purpose doesn't it?

UNCLE CECIL   I'm not a gentleman

AMELIA   You're not much good as a sex-slave neither.

UNCLE CECIL   Matron has no complaints.

CHORUS   All the nice boys love a sailor.

Enter MRS O'HARNESSEY   [in a sailor suit] You're nobody's sex-slave but mine.

   [She kneels down, displaying those strapping thighs, picks up Uncle Cecil by the scruff of his neck and carries him out.
   I don't think Mrs O is very polite barging in like that taking attention away from the Ghost of Barney Higgins.
(Though to be fair to her she hasn't shopped me as many times as Lushous Louise)

VOICE OF UNCLE CECIL   Don't think you've seen the last of me. I'm just lingering under the surface in a realm of shallow profundity.

The Hot Sheets Hotel

BARNEY   Under the covers, on the bed,
where love is done but never said.
Put down the notes, nothing's free,
that's the way with Billie and me.

BILLIE You think the bills pay themselves?

BARNEY [upon the entry of Portuguese Joe] Look who it is. I wonder what he's snivelling about today.

PORTUGUESE JOE At least I'm not Billie's booby.

BARNEY And his face bearing the shape of the last whore who sat on it.

SEVERAL BITCHES OF BRETWALDA Don't call us that!

BARNEY You called me Duckie.

CHIEF BITCH OF BRETWALDA Come on, girls, don't dilly dally with the likes of him. West Ham Intercity are here.

BARNEY I bet they wreck the place again.

BILLIE That was the Neighbourhood Watch. Just because they didn't get a group rate.

PORTUGUESE JOE [to me] When the wife's away….

BARNEY She gone on a retreat, if you don't mind, something like that.

PORTUGUESE JOE   Don't be vague about your wandering taig.

BARNEY   That's no way to talk about….Whatshername…

BILLIE   Harriet.

BARNEY   That's right, Harriet, my very own bugbear.

PORTUGUESE JOE   Who goes bump in the night.

BARNEY   How'd you know that?

[Joe taps his nose. Billie kicks off one of her high-heels. It flies through the air with the greatest of ease and hits him on the mouth.

My office

I've drawn in chalk on the wall the back of Jane Russell, I'm standing there imagining her turning round.

UNCLE CECIL   [entering unawares] you're sad.

BARNEY   What about the babes high-stepping through your imagination.

UNCLE CECIL   Well…. A stacked Sibyl in a domino mask was there when I woke up this morning but that's different. You really should try to broaden your horizons
   [he adds pointing at the drawing]

BARNEY   You're the one standing there with nothing on but your underpants.

UNCLE CECIL   What makes you think they're mine?

A VOICE   I've reason to believe they're not
   [says Constable Cisco of the Blonde Squad who slaps Uncle Cecil on the back so hard he coughs out a wet ball of unmentionables]
We've confiscated a load of Toni home perms and run in Elsie the Suicide Blonde but we're nowhere near the bottom of this outbreak.

Enter a lovely in black attire and short dark hair. Blimey, it's

MISS STARK   It's alright, constable, I'll take over.

CONSTABLE CISCO   Yes, Commander.

  [Stone the crows, I never knew she was an undercover copper]

COMMANDER STARK   I've been expecting you, Higgins. You're tricky but you can't elude me.

BARNEY   I'm here nearly every day.

COMMANDER STARK   A clever ruse, hiding in plain sight.
  [she stands in front of me, gives me the once-over with dull blue eyes]
How would you like to be the D.A. in my secret court?

CONSTABLE CISCO   Is that wise, Commander?

COMMANDER STARK   As long as the Blonde is still at large we need all the help we can get.

Cellar of the Blonde Squad

Notice on the wall: I'M THE D.A. AND DON'T YOU FORGET IT.

HARRIET [with bucket and mop] I can't see why I have to clean your office, you never were that fussy about cleanliness.

...[I point up at the notice. She goes out shaking her head]

Enter LUSHOUS LOUISE I'm not used to getting up before noon. Haven't had time for anything.

D.A. BARNEY Don't worry. Women with shaggy hair-do's don't look all that different in the morning especially when they sleep with their make-up on.

LUSHOUS LOUISE [sitting on my desk, leaning over] Here, let me straighten this dickie bow of yours. And whyever are you wearing that bobbie's helmet?

BARNEY Never mind. I've finally got rid of Uncle Cecil, he's on a boat to Yokohama. Where's that book in which I put down all my arrests and kidnappings?

LUSHOUS LOUISE   How the devil should I know?

D.A. BARNEY   'Cause you're my secretary, that's why.

  [Pity about Miss Adair]

LUSHOUS LOUISE   That's not what you told me on the couch last night. You said my job was to---

D.A. BARNEY   Alright, alright, I'll get Miss Beltone to do your filing for you.

Enter MISS BELTONE   It's remarkable how many departed spirits become Red Injuns or haunt the Himalayas.

  [She is alluding to last week's séance. It's bloody marvellous what people believe. I like it when the ladies play footsie or scratch my palm]

D.A. BARNEY   [to Miss Beltone] It is the earnest desire of the departed souls that you come here and do filing.

MISS BELTONE   I cannot ignore the orders of Fate so deftly conveyed by you, you big butch thing. But as a lady who lunches I can not do any actual work and I'd like to remind you of what you promised me when you took away my private fabrics to help with your enquiries—

D.A. BARNEY   Okay, okay, I'll get Dame Looney to be your p.a.

Enter DAME LOONEY   Good gracious, Barney, what's going on here?
   [She goes over to where Sleepy Sid is on his haunches in a glass case]
What's the reason for this?

D.A. BARNEY   [brushing away a crocodile tear]   I had to do it. You don't know how much it hurts me but poor Sleepy has gone prematurely senile

   [This is WooWang's doing. Once his bones have set in that position he intends to sell him to the Museum of the Macabre. I found him in the donjon below, brought him up here so he can at least see what's going on]

DAME LOONEY   [tapping the glass, smiling sadly]   You poor poor man. Cut down before your prime.
   [Sleepy was never destined to have a prime]
But look over there, look at D.A. Barney, your protector and friend and I hope you know even in your befuddled state that you are not alone.

[So, I give orders to Lushous Louise who gives them to Miss Beltone who passes then on to Dame Looney, by which time I've forgotten what I wanted in the first place. That's what is known as the chain of command. I got the idea for it when I was in the Army.

The only snag is that what for example started out as Send reinforcements were going to advance finishes up as Send three and fourpence we're going to a dance.

WooWang's alley

Poor Crusher lying face down in the alley, wiping his nose on the ground. When you're a derelict in today's harsh society nobody wants to know you.

I certainly wouldn't.

Look at that brazen hussy lifting his head with her boot. Look at her short shabby skirt and the ladders in her stockings over plump legs. Alright I suppose if you like that sort of thing.

I certainly do.

BILLIE   You've got a nerve lying down on the job.

THE CRUSHER   I'm keeping a low profile.

BILLIE   Whose profile is that?

BARNEY   [stepping out of the shadows] Mine.

BILLIE   There's no sign of WooWang.

BARNEY   Don't worry, it's all going to plan.

BILLIE   [looking up at the sky] Is that part of your plan?

BARNEY   It's only Uncle Cecil levitating.

  [Back from Yokohama]

BILLIE   What's he looking at?

  [A Dantesque underworld of shebeens, billy-goat crossings, bagheads, draggletails, distaff battle cruisers, abram men, staggering hopheads and wide-eyed scullery maids at area gates.
  The Panhandle according to Uncle Cecil]

BILLIE   Barney! There's somebody down there holding a crossbow.

[I look into Billie's eyes, as big and round as pennies. I see no fear there. All I see is resignation, despondency, confusion and a tendency to eat wine gums in bed.

Uncle Cecil comes crashing down, an arrow in his breast. I go up to him]

BARNEY   I told you before about all this hovering about. You nearly fell on Billie there. I shan't tell you again.

UNCE CECIL   Good, I was getting tired of it.

[A collie comes over, licks his face. Revived he gets up, brushes himself down and nobly invested in his plus fours and deerstalker he once more sets off to follow his private star]

THE CRUSHER   If I was hoovering I wouldn't wear stuff like that.

BILLIE   He was shot, wasn't he.

BARNEY   That's only WooWang, he don't like people flying over his airspace.

BILLIE   There he is, over there.

BARNEY   Come on, Crusher he wants you to help him with a little experiment.

THE CRUSHER   No, not me, please not me.

BARNEY   Alright then, come with me down to the docks, I'll tie you to an anchor and throw you over into the welcoming arms of the resident octopus that lives there.

   [I was almost proud of him. He stood the water torture for forty minutes before he was taken to Miss Wink's Private Lunatic Asylum.

Elsewhere in the Panhandle

As Lord Spender's favourite, Lady Broomhilda (aka Harriet) considered herself a social hostess, adept at giving parties and making matches.
   Though she had to stop that when the phosphorous got up her nose. Here's

LORD SPENDER   [gentry with a landed interest in thirteen acres of Norfolk bog] I have here, milady, oil to anoint you.

LADY BROOMHILDA   It's only what I deserve.

[But there's another side to Lady Broomhilda. In darkest Pandhandle there's a flop joint where she is preparing relics in conjunction with a Dr Lovelock, deputy medical officer to the Footstool.

[That's who he thinks he is, having been thrust to the edge of madness by constant nagging.
Harriet suspects Dr Lovelock is me (so do I) but she's bewildered by his medical manners]

BARNEY   Mrs O is quite distressed by the fact that Quean Anne's Footstool hasn't a single relic to its name.

[Apart from Uncle Cecil of course]

LADY BROOMHILDA   Quite so but you can't produce relics in a week. Martyrs and hermits, yes, but relics are like fine cheeses, they can't be rushed.

[The world can sometimes be a confusing place when you suddenly find yourself throttling your wife]

BARNEY   [as Dr Lovelock] My apologies, madam, but my poor lovesick hands could not resist placing diamonds on your hoary neck.

LADY BROOMHILDA   [her hard heart fluttering like a dovecote] I see no diamonds but I quite understand why men can not control themselves within the aura of my neck.

BARNEY   [aside, talking to the wall] Aye, that's where the mischief lies. 'Tis that sorcerous amulet hanging there.

LADY BROOMHILDA   [fingering the hair curler hanging by a piece of string down unto her breast] Mrs O'Harnessey must be patient.

BARNEY   She is not renowned for it

LADY BROOMHILDA   This is not for the likes of us. We must parley with Dr Dee who made the Shrine of Turin. I have his address up there.
   [she climbs a stepladder to access a book]
Dr Lovelock what on earth are doing lying on your back?

BARNEY   I'm only looking up your skirt.

LADY BROOMHILDA   I should be cross with you but I do understand the magnetic allure of my bum and its knickers. When for services rendered I permit Uncle Cecil to handwash my smalls he is almost agog with exhalation.

[Not him again. He's had the run of this play long enough. But you try to get rid of him. I've tried twice already]

BARNEY   I've noticed he's wearing an amulet too.

LADY BROOMHILDA   It's my signature taliswoman, it wards off arrows and hags.

BARNEY   Like Auntie Atlas?

[The Antichrist claims she was thrown out of a window but some say her defenestration is an urban myth and she spent the day at Lady Broomhilda's tea party]

LADY BROOMHILA   Not that I invited her. She came in dressed as a maid servant to serve the horse dovers. Being an experienced hostess I noticed her pinny was not properly ironed and her fingernails painted black to hide the dirt. When I told her to discreetly depart she made the milk go sour.
   [She turns to Lord Spender]
Here, what's in this oil? It don't half pong.

LORD SPENDER   Just the boiled viscera of a gallows stiff, milady. [he holds up mirror] See, it's working already.

LADY BROOMHILDA   Yes, I've always wanted a widow's peak.

A STRANGE VOICE   Not so fast
  [says a dog-faced baboon called Herman. There are three of them. They move across the room on all fours, raising their hats.

THE THREE BABOONS   Hear no evil, see no evil, speak no evil.

LORD SPENDER   It is poignant to think these creatures were once men.

Cellar of the Blonde Squad

HARRIET [putting down her mop] Show kindness to your dutiful wife and let me confess my sins too. [Starts to sing] Straight from my heart I cry to thee, Barney, Barney, hear my plea.

D.A. BARNEY   There's a confession box at the door. Use it.

[She exits. Billie comes in, stands abashed in front of my desk]

D.A. BARNEY   Before I send you over, angel, I want you to know I could have fallen for you big time, but I won't play the sap for you.

BILLIE   [nervous laugh] You're kidding aren't you? Tell me you're kidding.
   [Long pause]
But you're human, Barney, tell me you're human.

D.A. BARNEY   I suppose I am.

BILLIE   Give me a cigarette

D.A. BARNEY   [taking a long pull on my Camel] I don't smoke.

   [She starts gubbing. I'm not a D.A. who worries about dames who gub. I go into the small room where I keep my instruments, close the door. I peer into the periscope I've installed to look into Commander Stark's changing room. I hear my prisoner crying]

BILLIE   How can you do such a thing?

On the street

I'm talking to the wall again. I tell it about strapping games mistresses, highly strung horsewomen, short-skirted skaters, jumping volleyball players. Add blondes according to taste and you have a dish fit for

DAVE KING   About time you brought me into it.

BARNEY   I didn't think you cared.

DAVE KING   I'm the quid for your quo.

BARNEY   I thought Dr Lovelock was.

DAVE KING   Dr Lovelock be damned. I'm the acceptable face of Barney Higgins, not him. And certainly not you.

BARNEY   The Squire has multiple personalities but I don't think I have, although I can't be sure if they don't know about each other.

DAVE KING   You've never liked me, have you? I can sing, dance, crack good jokes. And what are you? A broken down bricklayer. No wonder Commander Stark gave you the boot.

[I may not have mentioned that. Some unpleasantness over a periscope.
Dave King takes it on his toes and I hear the footfall of a witch]

AUNTIE ATLAS   Woe is me.

BARNEY   What are you whining about now?

AUNTIE ATLAS   Oh, Barney, a double catastrophe has overcome me. I let the Cranky Wee Brat of the SNP live under my bed and now, lo and behold, I find there's a whole mess of them, squealing and moaning.
So I fly out of my bat cave and there down in the valley a giant penis rises from the ground. Too, too dazzling for a poor spinster's sight.

BARNEY   Come off it, you know the Americans are down there, what you saw was a missile coming out of a silo, and if you want a shag you only have to ask for one.

AUNTIE ATLAS   Now that you mention it, I am on the pill.

[You'd have to boil her first]

BARNEY   Watch out, here comes a patrol.

[We merge into the shadows as a troop of Girl Guides march by

SINGING   We love to go a-wandering….

BARNEY   Phew, that was close.

AUNTIE ATLAS   Come on, Barney, cut out the cant and tell me how much you pine for me.

[And there, before my very eyes, Auntie transforms herself into a pair of black tights, the mound of her pudendum looks me straight in the eye and says

EXTERNAL GENITAL ORGAN   L'etat c'est moi.

The British Massage Parlour Inspectorate

has employed me to carry out an investigation.

THE ONE-ARMED MAN   Eddie was my d-d-downfall and to make a short story long I lay down on a table and watched her rub my dong—

BARNEY   [to Eddie]   What have you got to say for yourself?

EDDIE   [Lady Fivefingers]   Well, he's right-handed and he lost it at sea.

BARNEY   When I enter a massage parlour I look at whether there's too much hygiene for a nostalgie de la boue qualification, whether the masseuse's table manners are sufficiently shameless and whether there are available, for those customers sexually fixated in the Fifties, a supply of tan stockings and face powder.

THE ONE-ARMED MAN   Auntie Atlas c-c-called me in, gave me cream out of her big tin, half a tit with sugar on the top and two black balls out of her wee shop.

BARNEY   She's been under investigation for imposing a wanking tax on unauthorised domestic activity. By the way, who is that nut over there?

EDDIE   Can't you tell O'Rourke from his stutter?

BARNEY   I remember him now, but he didn't have a stutter.

EDDIE   That was before. He told Auntie he'd give his right arm for a night of bliss.

BARNEY   Careless talk costs arms.

EDDIE   That was a false arm, anyway.

[What a cheat! Fancy complaining he lost his arm. In my life there have been many women, strange and wonderful and grasping and I could say they've cost me an arm and a leg but I begrudge them nothing.
   I've never liked O'Rourke. Red-headed, a southpaw and a face like a smacked arse….What more is there to dislike?
   There's plenty. But nobody's blameless and we'd better let him pass for what he's worth.
   Which isn't much. I remember when he and his navvies ran amok in the Tabard Inn in Torquay. They were lucky the plod stayed away.
   As usual, which is why more landlords are keeping Alsatians behind the bar.
   But I'm getting too political here, so I'll just tell you that a suspender-belted Eddie has passed the nostalgie de la boue test, displaying a fine run in her fully-flavoured, fully-fashioned tan stockings]

Quean Anne's Footstool

It was always a sore point with Matron [bless her jealous heart] that Amelia had a chain-gang and the Footstool had not.
   So she rounded up some of my Ancient Mariners.

MATRON   ...and you will pay proper respect to your foreman, Barney Higgins.

   [it's only what I deserve]

BARNEY   Listen up you rag tags and bobtails, yes you are the rabbits and I am the weasel.
   [I like to show off my metaphors at times like this]
Matron has put you in this inaugural chain-gang because of your history of sex scandals. You think you're all Tory MPs now, is that it?

MEMBER OF CHAIN GANG   And we're not district attorneys neither.

   [What a thing to say!]

BARNEY   Wait a minute, I know you
   [Blow me down if it's not Mr Pastry]

What you doing here when you should be hibernating?

MRS PASTRY Miss Stark hired me out to clean this massive pile , it was damp and had it's own asylum where they kept the inbreds and poor girls who were inconvenient. And fat fruits waddling about the halls in tight trousers. We called it the Petrified City.

BARNEY News to me.

MR PASTRY Also known as Buckingham Palace.

BARNEY You insolent pup. Have you never heard the expression Out of the frying pan into the fire?

MR PASTRY I say phooey to your fire.

MATRON Enough! Don't bandy words with Foreman Barney.

BARNEY It would help if I could have a horse, a shotgun and dark glasses.

MATRON Don't be presumptuous. You may be foreman but you're still a member of the chain-gang.

[So here am I holding the wrong end of the stick again.
Though it depends on how you look at it.
I always look on the distaff side of life.
Even now as Matron strides out in her jodhpurs I've never seen her breasts so high or her lips so pursed]

Botany Bay

UNCLE CECIL   Can I be one of the warders?

MATRON   It seems obsequiousness is not your forte. You must work harder at it, and who knows, some day you may have a uniform.

UNCLE CECIL   With a cap too?

MATRON   Don't be presumptuous. Now, I've secured a contract to clear Anthrax Island of its dead sheep and asbestos. Have the chain-gang loaded up and ready.

[I let out the breath I'm holding for extra sprinting power, rise up and trip over my chain. Matron comes over, pushes my face into the mud with her boot]

MATRON   I have my Procrustean methods for dealing with escapers.

UNCLE CECIL   Give him the jolts.

MATRON   Good idea. I haven't yet used that electric chair you invented.
  [She summons the rest of the chain-gang who are hiding in the trees]
Take Uncle Cecil and let him be the first to try out his electric chair.
  [She says to me]
Let this be a lesson to both of you. Never be sure of what a woman will do next. I expect you'll be wanting a cup of tea after your abortive exertions

  [She can rub it in alright, but fingers crossed, this could be the last we'll see of Uncle Cecil]

PART four

Quean Anne's Footstool

I've just left Harriet. She has on her booze-blossomed face a smile of revengeful satisfaction. I wonder what's up.

MRS O'HARNESSEY   O woe is me. My nemesis is come. [On her knees, wringing her hands] In dread I've waited for years and years. The curse of the elephant idol is upon me. All I did was sit on it.

BARNEY   Elephants do not forget. You must make amends.

MRS O'HARNESSEY   I don't deserve these amends. I shall redeem myself like Profumo with good works.

BARNEY   Profumo can not save you.

  [Mrs O sobs and cries. After a while she says

MRS O'HARNESSEY   But what can save me?

BARNEY   Lure Uncle Cecil here, make him a doormat so you can stamp out your guilt.

MRS O'HARNESSEY   I never liked him anyway.

BARNEY   And you must pay penance, just to pass yourself in the eyes of the idol. You must walk the length of Knightsbridge in your nightgown.

   [As I leave I notice a hair-curler on the sideboard. Lady Broomhilda's calling card, like the Lone Ranger's silver bullet]

Harriet won her case for desertion and I get put back on the Cruel Husbands Register, and in case you haven't heard, I'm also the world's greatest liar.
   But is it any wonder I'm never there. Dishes stacked, stuff all over the floors and sore points laid throughout like mines.
   Just imagine if I did clean and housekeep:

HARRIET   [to her kitchen cabinet] It's only Betty doing women's work.

MRS O'HARNESSEY   My chambermaids and laundresses would like their own skivvy. I shall call her Abigail.

BILLIE [standing close, the butt in her mouth singeing my nose] I shall call you Molly. I'll beat as you sweep as you clean.

   [I may find her hot smoky breath abnormally erotic but I steady myself, hold my head up and try to be proud.
   If only this danged corset wouldn't dig into me. Believe it or not, it's medicinal for my bad back]

BARNEY I aint gonna work on Emma's Farm no more.

BILLIE What's she on about?

HARRIET Who could heed her.

   [Once you start helping round the house you could finish up like

SLEEPY SID [dancing in, wearing a tutu with spangles and sequins] Lavender's blue, dilly dilly, lavender's green, when you are king, dilly dilly, I'll be your queen.

   [There's no way back from there]

The Agony of St Agnes

THE BLONDE   In my religion we don't find womanly forms offensive. We don't cover them up like lepers.

BIG JACK BRAG   [having lost his pillion pussy] Has anyone here seen Harriet, Harriet from the Emerald Isle?

[You remember the time Father McGillicuddy roared up on his Norton with Harriet's arms round him?
  No, neither do I, but it must have happened because she still talks about it in her sleep.
  So Big Jack Brag tells us.
  He heard it from Portuguese Joe]

THE BLONDE   You should address me as the Loved One.

BIG JACK BRAG   Take a ride with me. Cisco can't keep up.

THE BLONDE   Barney, someone somewhere wants a dig in the beak from you.

BARNEY   The Loved One likes people to be polite to her.

[I sock him on the ear, he flies back against the wall, then with his cheek against it, his mouth open, he slides down it until he's resting on his knees, trying to suck in air.

THE BLONDE   Watch yourself with him.

BARNEY   Holds grudges, does he.

THE BLONDE   You'll never be safe.

BARNEY   Take care of him permanent?

[The Blonde nods and there's a very alarmed look on his face as I help him up by his tie, I pull out my revolver, shove the muzzle in his mouth. The poor sod's terrified, I can hear his teeth hitting against the metal of the pistol]

BARNEY   So long, sucker.

[I squeeze the trigger, three clicks can be heard above the sound of him wetting himself]

The Seven Stars

Cardiac unit

BARNEY   A pint of your best bilge water.

THE REV BROCKLEHURST   [hand on heart] Blessed are the pacemakers and the buxom big-bottomed nurses. Give me a gin and orange.

   [A more experienced degenerate would have seen through those saucy ministering angels with over-priced legs and greedy hands clutching hypodermics. He'll find out when he tries to pay for the drink. But it's probably just as well, seeing how the gin could well be methanol from China.

UNCLE CECIL   It was clever of you, Barney, to get me off. Make 'em think I'm a halfwit controlled by Big Jack Brag.

   [Inspector Gorse and his men had come to arrest him for making bribes to Special Branch. Instead of to them]

A VOICE   [in my ear, hand on crotch]   Schh….you know who this is…let my fingers do the wanking.

[Its Lushous Louise. This is outrageous stuff, but it doesn't matter, only an unlucky few will get to read it.
She realizes I'm spent, she turns to the vicar

LUSHOUS LOUISE   Get your spondulics out.

THE REV BROCKLEHURST   Alas, dear lady, my nocky boy is sleeping and one of your nurses has relieved me of my scratch.

BARNEY   Watch it, this is Miss Wink you're talking to.

THE REV BROCKLEHURST   Yes, news of her appointment did reach me at my vicarage. The Gentleman Caller was leaving off some stuff and he let me know.

[The Gentleman Caller is a burglar and con-man, he even had a go at being the Tichborne Claimant and his project only failed because he was one hundred years out of date.
Lushous Louise call it a night?

LUSHOUS LOUISE   Not on your Nellie…..Uncle Cecil, will you walk into my parlour….

UNCLE CECIL   Said the spider to the fly. I should be highly honoured,

noble lady
   [he says, bowing with a gravity that does him proud, and after she puts her hand in his pocket and pulls out his wallet they stroll off arm in arm, displaying the chic appropriate to a decomposing nabob and his paid companion]

Emma's Farm

Who is Emma, what is she?
I don't know but I'm now foreman over her serfs.

HARRIET   I know farms nowadays have to find other forms of income but what you're doing with those serfs is unbecoming.

BARNEY   They have to earn their keep.

HARRIET   Hanging them up as punchbags at a dollar a thump?

BARNEY   For wives only. They can pretend it's their husband.

HARRIET   And hiring them out as tailors' dummies or stood standing in shop windows.

BARNEY Needles and pins, needles and pins, when a man marries his trouble begins.

HARRIET Don't change the subject. You're always out to use people, even your own children. You told them to save up for their holidays. I couldn't believe it when I saw them putting their shillings in the gas meter.

Enter BILLIE [fuming and terrible as an army with maypoles] O daft Barney whom nobody loves, why did you pay Eddie to take off her gloves?

HARRIET That's him all over. First it's my gloves, then yours, then Eddie's. Where's it gonna end?

BILLIE In tears, I suppose.

BARNEY Never mind that. Who is this Emma?

BILLIE Her story's this. Born of shabby genteel lace-curtain Irish she fled to Soho and there clad in the blue dress of ignominy she was rampant like a beast beating the air, her well-fed thighs going unnoticed until she lifted up her hems.

HARRIET I know how she felt. It's not nice to be taken for granted.

   [I make bold to say

BARNEY How many Emmas are there?

BILLIE As many as there are burdens left by biblecarriers and greybeards of medieval bent.

I walk into this farmhouse. On the wall there is a panoply of Emma and all her works. Excerpts from the *Book of Emma 22*, pictures of life under the cat's foot, and a selection of her early panties.

EDDIE We need a butler here. What about Higgins?

HARRIET Won't do. He's not house-trained.

BILLIE To quick on the zipper if you ask me.

HARRIET He'd only be casing the joint.

BILLIE   Hand over the dosh you made from them serfs.

   [The three dames flare up a bit as an elusive butterfly appears and flutters over their heads]

THE WITCH OF WOOKEY   Help me, Barney, help me.

BARNEY   What is it this time?

THE WITCH OF WOOKEY   I need someone to take my place in the unhappy hunting ground. Any would-be martyr will do.

   [I look at

HARRIET   Father McGillicuddy said I was already a martyr being married to you.

BILLIE   Martyrs are so self-indulgent.

EDDIE   Barney, follow me and I'll show you my new girdle.

   [Three dames exit speedily.
   Madame Mao enters.

I point at O'Rourke who thinks I can't see him pretending to be a statue of a bog labourer digging at the turf]

O'ROURKE   Not me, I'm not ready yet.

MADAME MAO   La mort ne surprend point le sage, il est toujours pret a partir.

[Death does not surprise the wise man, he is always ready to go.
I nod sorrowfully]

The three layers of Limbo

The first was founded in the 14th century by Higgins the Hateful who had borrowed money to be repaid in the afterlife so he was quite happy to stay where his was having a few jars at the Tabard Inn with

G CHAUCER   This world nis but a thurghfare ful of wo, and we ben pigrimes passinge to and fro, deeth is an ende of every worldly sore.

HIGGINS THE HATEFUL   Such a cheery fellow you are.

G CHAUCER   Thou shalt make castels than in Spayne and dream of joye al but in vayne.

BAAL'S FIRES   [an abstraction] I have news for you ghouls

[Chaucer's little pig eyes cloud over, his chin starts to quiver. He's not only snivelling, he's melting. That's because he's made of wax. All that's left is a pair of teeth]

EDITH OF NANCY TOWN   You'll wonder where the yellow went when you brush your teeth with Pepsident.

[This is bizarre but freedom of expression and liberty go together]

CHORUS   You can't have one without the other.

In the second layer there are in the region of thirty to forty well-upholstered doxies.

HIGGINS THE HANDFUL   Which is a very good region to be in.

SAINT JUDE   [patron saint of lost causes] Look who it is.

JOSEF STALIN   [whispering through the keyhole of his darkness] Of all the treasures a state can possess, the human lives of its citizens are for us the most precious.

[Such an excellent libel. The ghoul of ghouls would never say that.
But he did]

The ides of

MARTHA   [poor woman's Mandy Rice Davies] Who let in these cuckoos? Not one of them can be trusted to say his prayers at night.

DAVY JONES   That's old school. Nobody's listening.

MRS ROUNCIVAL   I'd listen. I can't do anything but they can promise to worship me and appreciate the beauty of my aroma.

MRS GRUNDY   It is a great comfort to me, Higgins the Handful, to see you there, chained to the mast of the celestial Ship of Shame.

The third came into place in the realm of Queen Betty and we see Tom Tug going at it ding dong with the Alderman but it's more dong than ding as the pair of them lie on both sides of the pillow.

TOM TUG   I claim the Portsmouth Defence.

HIGGINS THE HURTFUL   Your way of sin is too broad for me.

MRS GRUNDY   [calling us together for a glimpse of the future] I see the entire infrastructure of this Great Britain in the hands of the foreigner, I see murderers let out of prison after six years (so they can kill again) and I see people taking holidays in Turkey.

PETER PIEMAN   Stay away from turkey. Doesn't mix with pastry.

JACK PUDDING   What's wrong with black pudding?

Never on a Sunday says Mrs Grundy.

BILLY SHAKES   To durst or not to durst.

MADAME MAO   [to Jack Pudding] Revenons a nos moutons.

[Don't change the subject, we're talking turkey here]

HIGGINS THE HURTFUL   Sheep or turkeys, you can't have it both ways.

[That does it. Madame Mao immerses him in the juices of her sweat drenched witches and Higgins the Hurtful is now only a ripple murmuring goodbye

The mare's nest

Where dreams go horribly wrong.

STRADIVARIUS   You've been claiming for years that that old mandolin-banjo of yours was made by me. So be it. Now we shall turn our hands to mandolin-banjos and you shall be the toast of Vienna.

BARNEY   It's only what I deserve.

STRADIVARIUS   It's the least I can do for the man who has ruined my reputation.

BARNEY   [to Harriet] You've been having bad thoughts about your poor husband.

HARRIET   I was only throttling him
  [she cries and rushes away to hide in the wardrobe strategically placed for runaway wives.
  In which there is an enchantment which has her walking the plank and falling into a shoal of octopuses.
  I'm stepping over Slippery Sam with blood all over like strawberry jam.
  Here's Constable Cisco whom you've met before, averting his eyes from Slippery's gore. As a copper he's well below par but he does wear pink panties and a Playtex bra]

CONSTABLE CISCO   If you want to know the time or who did the crime, don't ask a policeman.

  [Taffy was a Welshman, Taffy was not a thief. He didn't come to your station to steal a joint of beef.
  Was those Jacobites, I shouldn't wonder.
  Could never take no for an answer]

CONSTABLE CISCO   But we all have our broken dreams.

BARNEY   That's what the sea lords said before they sailed away tp Canada to escape the Russians and Chinese and to set up a Royal Navy in exile.

CONSTABLE CISCO   How many ships does the Navy have?

BARNEY   Just the two they were on. But they're good ones, they made them to last in 1914.

   [Suddenly the lights dim. Shapes and five o'clock shadows creep across the stone walls.
   There's a dramatic freeze. Stradivarius, Harriet and Cisco are conserved in aspic and the copper's boot is caught in mid-air]

Norfolk Island

Harriet has escaped from the wardrobe and to her credit holds against me no more recrimination than usual.
   I think she still fancies me.
   I call it the dark side of love.

HARRIET   I'd rather roll in a bed of nettles. No, make that thorns.

   [Here's

MATRON   [pushing the Crusher in front of her]   I knelt down to say my prayers and I found this creature under the bed
   [she tells us and zaps him with a taser. He falls on his back clutching his chest]

Enter INSPECTOR GORSE   Just ignore him. They do that when we zap them too.

   [But Matron is made of kinder stuff. She sits on his chest, bounces up and down until his ticker fires up again.
   I hear puffing and plodding. I look up to see

CLOTHILDA   [the fattest woman to ever sail round the world]   I bring tidings of great moment.

   [A pause while she gets her breath back]

BARNEY   Well, what is it?

CLOTHILDA   Horace Himmler and me now control this island and all its slave workers -including you- and so we can start to build our wonder weapons.

   [I may have been a slave worker on Emma's Farm but I'm not having this.
   I quickly disable Clothilda by pulling off her wig]

BARNEY   Come, Harriet dear, we must be going. I have a raft waiting.

HARRIET   No I must stay. Clothilda needs me. I am her bit of fluff.

BARNEY   Well, I'll be gormed. You never really know people, do you? Even after all these years.

HARRIET   We don't even know ourselves.

Alimonia

There's a coal mine here. Closed down by Government fiat. They want us to freeze in the dark.

CONSTABLE CISCO   We coulda had a police state by now if my fellow bluebottles weren't so inherently idle.

[that's where P.C. is leading us.
So her mine has been converted into a mental home and she takes patient welfare very seriously]

AMELIA   [to Uncle Cecil, Chief of Security]   Blow the entrance to the mine.

[He orders his white trash to do that but it's not long before the miners – if I may call them that, I prefer it to "conceptually challenged" – come clambering up through the rabble.

BARNEY   Leave it to Captain Moonlight.
   [I run towards them, shake my fist]
Back you loonies, back.

[Yes, it's dangerous but I don't care. A clod of turf hits me right on the smacker. I push my glasses back on my nose, walk defiantly back]

At the pineapple

As told to me by Sleepy Sid

FATHER McGILLICUDDY   [in his pulpit] That celebrated explorer Barney Higgins is just back from Patagonia where he was looking for Major Fawcett. And I would like to remind everyone to be careful as there is more crime about than ever before.

   [Patagonia is the local cant word for prison]

SLEEPY SID   Boy, will that give those bitches on Harriet's Round Table something to rabbit about.
   [Did he say Harriet's?]
Well, yes….

HARRIET   Never mind, you don't know what women talk about.

SLEEPY SID   Honest men are better off not knowing that.

   [At which point she notices the priest rubbing the inside of his cassock, puts her hand over her mouth, screams]

Madam GeeGee's Chamber of Horrors

Here I am being stroked by the fragrant fingers of a doxie with dragon-lady eyes. The hour is struck. At the tenth dong a baldy old coot steps out of the grandfathers clock.

UNCLE CECIL   Freeze you heroes.
   [Madam gives a pretendy scream]
Once more into the jaws of the honey-trap treads the fearless agent.

MADAM   Not tonight he doesn't.

UNCLE CECIL   Ah don't be pedantic. What about some small suggestive talk to begin with.

MADAM   No.

UNCLE CECIL   A dog must be bad indeed who is not worthy of a bone.

   [Sighing, Madam gets up, takes the dog collar from around my neck, puts it on

UNCLE CECIL   You're an effing old cow.

   [A red-tipped finger moves again, presses a button and Harriet the Stepford Wife emerges]

UNCLE CECIL   And Higgins can't count neither. Unless he uses his fingers.

   [I feel like giving him one. But my hands are tied. To the legs of a table]

MADAM   [to Harriet] The order of the boot.
   [who kicks the old reprobate in the whatsits]
Now get back under the table.
   [Harriet does so in a mechanical fashion and Madam strolls around the chamber]
I am beginning to think my agents have failed me.

BARNEY AND UNCLE CECIL   We wouldn't dare, Madam GeeGee.

MADAM   No more will my riff and raff defy me. I shall skin my agents into deeper modes of devotion and cause stampedes in their hearts with one beckoning gesture of this red-tipped finger...

As for you, yellowbelly [she says to Portuguese Joe who is standing to attention in the Cryptic Corner wearing his Prushun helmet with a spike on top and holding a wooden rifle] you are too fat and will henceforth live on char and wads – with margarine of course.

Because giving butter to a wretch like you is as inconceivable as you being kissed and cuddled by a decent dominatrix.

[She turns towards us]
What say you, Uncle Cesspit?

UNCLE CECIL   Hi de hi.

HARRIET   [in automatic response mode]   Ho de ho.

UNCLE CECIL   I spent happy days with spiteful old crones and lepers. I wasn't allowed butter neither. They wanted my nose but I outsmarted them and they settled for just three of my toes.

[Don't admire him too much. As a Cossack he blotted his copy book forcing Kulaks into cattle cars. So he tells me]

MADAM   Enough! I am not interested in your operations.

[Us exhibits freeze. She goes around moving an arm here, a head there, until we're just as she wants us]

MADAM   This world really is an absurd place, isn't it?

It certainly was when the Ancient Mariners of all people went on the rampage. Now, wrecking the police station is one thing, looting Mrs O's guest house is quite another.
   Her trainee tarts who were practicing on the lodgers were terrified. So were the coppers.
   They were the lodgers.
   They had it cushy in that station, watching game shows and playing darts but a new young inspector made life difficult for them.

SERGEANT BLUEBOTTLE   He'll learn.

   [I'm the only lodger who isn't evicted to make room for extra Peelers and I'm not at all pleased when Little Lily Bullero makes a fuss of them at breakfast giving them more fry than I get.

MRS O'HARNESSEY   Don't be picky. And don't rub them Peelers the wrong way.

   [She even lets them call her Sally which is forbidden to the likes of you and me. Lord Spender of Grubstreet pushes his luck. He calls call her that at

Miss Wink's Supper Rooms at the Academy

I hear it. Harriet is giving a talk on matrimonial torment and I stand there as an example of what to avoid. The lecture attracts Ester the chemist from Cologne. Like a shark to a lump of meat. She sinks her teeth into my neck.

HARRIET [kicking me on the shin] Higgins, let go of that woman.

ESTER Yes, Barney, you are a terrible nuisance to us womens.

MRS O'HARNESSEY He should be brought up before the Committee of Matrons, of which of course I am the supreme matron with a lamp.

LORD SPENDER And I am your humble stretcher bearer. Clad only in my robes and a laurel wreath, comme it faut.

HARRIET We thank ee m'lud but we poor stalwarts are only educated beggars who know nothing of your Roman tongue.

BARNEY   I was brought in front of that committee before and I'm not going back.

HARRIET   You'll do as you're told.

BARNEY   Talk about being literal. I had to jump through actual hoops.

MRS O'HARNESSEY   You must have got Matron Merkel. She has refined schadenfreude to a new peak.

BARNEY   Is that the same as strangling patients with their own bow-tie?

MRS O'HARNESSEY   Now, now, Barney, I've told you before, a healthy fetishism keeps a man virile in later life.

BARNEY   I'm not that old.

MRS O'HARNESSEY   Ancient brains can be imaginative because they have a lot of experience to draw upon.

Enter UNCLE CECIL   If they're too ancient they go backwards. I should know, I'm on my second honeymoon.

HARRIET It used to be when old geezers was doting they just sat in the corner drooling and giggling, smoking their pipes and talking nonsense, looked after by their family. Now they call it big words and put them in smelly homes run by forriners.

[Silence hangs]

MRS O'HARNESSEY Don't look at me. I'm not a forriner. And I change the bath water at least once a week.

BARNEY How comes it then that you confiscate their teeth?

UNCLE CECIL Yes, but to be fair she does rent them back to us during the day.

MRS O'HARNESSEY A mere service charge. At my retirement home we take patient safety very seriously and so we make sure they don't choke on them in their sleep. Of course one may moderate one's professional impulses with a natural self-interest.

LORD SPENDER As a mere stretcher-bearer may I have the temerity to nominate you for another lamp?

MRS O'HARNESSEY It's only what I deserve.

[stepping forward, pointing dramatically]
Particularly having to put up with Uncle Cesspit.

[but he's not bothered, he does a little jig then presents us with his backside]

MRS O'HARNESSEY   Them girls at my high-class convent come psalm singing twice a week to attend my patients, and this old fart tells them he's bound up and needs a greasy finger up his ancient causeway.

HARRIET   It's against natcher if you ask me.

BARNEY   Why is he wearing a white nightgown and cap at this time of day?

PORTUGUESE JOE   [his chief features emerging from the end of a cardboard box that is assuming the shape of a parallelogram as Mrs O sits on it]   I hope he's not the Holy Maid of Kent again.

MRS O'HARNESSEY   Who asked you, get back in there.
  [she claps her hands, Muldoon and Bucky Buchanan march in]
Keep in step, keep in step.

[To the surprise of the company they arrest Lord Spender, take him out]

Punishment chamber at the Footstool

Lord Spender is sulking in a cage of little ease.
 Mrs O is cutting her initials on a dead slave.

BARNEY   You should do that to live ones so that if they abscond and get caught the New Gestapo will who they belong to.

MRS O'HARNESSEY   That's academic. None dare defy the power of my supremacy.

 [She's just sore 'cause she didn't think of it first]

Enter THE GREAT PANJANDRUM   [the Footstool's spellbinder. He waves Mrs O away, says to Harriet who is hiding in the corner]   Come with me to Spanish Town. You too, Higgins.

BARNEY   I told you we would go places.

HARRIET   That was twenty years ago and where have I been?

BARNEY   You've been to Wales and Brighton.

HARRIET   Only because you had me kidnapped.

PORTUGUESE JOE   Take me with you
  [he says, climbing out of his cardboard box in his birthday suit]

BARNEY   I'll never eat a cold frankfurter again.

HARRIET   If I'd known he was like this I'd never have let him live under my table.

THE GREAT PANJANDRUM   Hush, hush, sweet Harriet. When you was the Conductress---

BARNEY   The original Conductress if you don't mind.

THE GREAT PANJANDRUM   …you displayed yourself too.

HARRIET   Stockings and suspenders is different.

THE GREAT PANJANDRUM   Eh lass, I wasn't criticising you. Walking up and down those steps was the pinnacle of your perfidious existence.

HARRIET   [feeling gratified and slightly nervous] Thank you, sir, but I have to go home now and make my husband's tea.

The Footstool

The chair of the Committee of Matrons is occupied by the wobblised buttocks of Matron Merkel. Even now she can hear faint echoes of the bells ringing as her ancestors ravished Paris in 1871.
　But that's nothing. Gerry went on to far bigger and bitter destructions than that.

MATRON MERKEL   To protect the people's new-found freedom we have formed a secret police with it's own secret court.

　[Here's my solicitor, Vera Vamp, the Blonde Beast. She's pulling me along with a rope round my neck]

VERA VAMP   Don't be too hard on him. A year in the punishment chamber should be enough to reconstruct him.

MATRON MERKEL   Your defence is elegant. But quite useless. The rule of 1984 provides for---

VERA VAMP   Yes, for ever. But as a good lesbian you don't want to pre-judge the future. I mean, who ever would have thought of hooped petticoats making a comeback?

BARNEY   What was once will come again. I expect it'll be bodices next.

VERA VAMP   There, you see. Barney will emerge from the dungeon depths as a fully-formed suffragette.

MATRON MERKEL   Yes, I see it all now. And he shall be called Dopey Dora.

BARNEY   I prefer Nancy Nutmeg.

MATRON MERKEL   Really! I must protest.

[You may be wondering how I've fallen down so much. Or you may not. I'll tell you anyway. I'm undercover for the Way of the Arch, the English resistance.
  Sounds important, don't it? Harriet thinks so. But I know better.

I know where I am and how I got here. By dint of some hard double-crossing, greed, duplicity and disregard for the welfare of others I have transformed myself from a foreman bricklayer into a shyster snooper who feeds off undercover scraps for a bunch of losers.

You remember the Squire and his multiple personalities. At present he's Pancho the First except when he's a Tolpuddle martyr.

That's when Basher, passing in his mobile asylum, gives him a lift to Quean Anne's Footstool where Harriet is waiting with her second-best umbrella.

PANCHO THE FIRST   Ah Lady Broomhilda, most beloved of strumpets
   [he cries as Harriet gives him one]
Can this be a harbinger of future endearments?

HARRIET   Where's the Squire, where's my money?

PANCHO THE FIRST   He is about, dear lady, so I have been informed by the ancient annals Hippopotumus himself....
   [He gets another whack]
And by the memoirs of the venerable Ogham...
   [Another one]

And by the deeds of Killiecrankie where I rescued a certain Mrs Grundy and restored to her all her father's teaspoons.

HARRIET   You met Mrs Grundy? Oh your majesty.

  [She kneels down in homage and unlaces his boots.
  Pancho goes back to biting his nails.
  All this time I have been standing inside a statue of the Great Panjandrum sent down specially by Securicor from oop north. Those two have been ignoring me since they came in. I thought they might. I think that when you look like an exhibit in a black museum people should pay more attention to you.
  Heralded by a blast from a rolled-up newspaper the Quean of Diamonds enters. Pancho jumps out of his boots, rushes over to her, licks her proffered hand]

Enter UNCLE CECIL   [with the New Gestapo] That beats Banagher.

  [The said Banagher (another of the Squire's personalities) goes white and then, like a bolt from the blue, he bolts.
  But he's hauled back by the New Gestapo, who have forearms like Popeye. They throw him up in the air]

THE QUEAN OF DIAMONDS   [looking down at the writhing Banagher]

Don't take on so. The meat wagon will be here presently.
  [She sees Harriet]
And take her too. That overweight replica of....

BARNEY   Joan Crawford
  [I offer from inside the statue]

THE QUEAN OF DIAMONDS   That's right. She's like an overweight Joan Crawford.
  [She looks around]
Who said that?

  [But I keep schtum. I think about my poor wife being put into dog food...But not for long, not being prone to morbid sentimentality]

THE QUEAN OF DIAMONDS   [stamping her foot in anger]
I said, Who said that?

Checkpoint Charlie

UNCLE CECIL   Barney, get me down, I don't like it up here.

BARNEY You got up, you get down. You don't have the makings of a pillar saint.

AUNT CECILIA Get you down from that chimbley at once.

BARNEY Light a fire in there, that'll shift him.

HARRIET See how clever Barney is.

BARNEY You're still not getting that stuff. They send out those catalogues to tempt women and put them in debt.

HARRIET What about---

BARNEY Underwear is different.

   [Sound of cawing above.
   See the Antichrist coming down with her rooks...]

AUNTIE ATLAS Come unto me all ye who are round-shouldered and have sand kicked in your faces...

   [...and watch those rooks peck at Uncle Cecil until he jumps]

141

Later

LEAMAS   They tell me this is a safe house.

BARNEY   Not quite. There's a loose floorboard in the kitchen.

UNCLE CECIL   You can always tell a City & Guilds man.

LEAMAS   Both the Chinese and North Koreans are after the Pyramid, a device of so vile intention that no honest man can experience it and stay sane.

  [There's an implication hanging in the air but I ignore it]

BARNEY   Yes it was a Tasmanian time for Captain Moonlight.

UNCLE CECIL   [to Leamas] That's his other monica.

BARNEY   Ignore him. He fell from a chimney and bruised his cortex, which wasn't strong at the best of times.

UNCLE CECIL   I won't say I'm unbalanced, just a little unhinged.

LEAMAS   I take my hat off to you, Barney, as the Pyramid's only known survivor [aside to Uncle Cecil] Is he always like this?

UNCLE CECIL   This is him on a good day.

BARNEY   I heard that.

LEAMAS   Tell me, Uncle Cecil, why are you wearing a kilt?

UNCLE CECIL   Auntie Atlas wants all men to wear one.

BARNEY   She's turned his head. Last week he was one of those ecstatics lying in a trench, calling up the King of Hell.

UNCLE CECIL   Careful, wolves have ears.

BARNEY   Look at his trembling knees.

   [Enter Aunt Cecilia. She grabs Uncle Cecil by the ear, pulls him out]

AUNT CECILIA   I'm disgraced again.

BARNEY It's her own fault. She only beats him once a month.

[Leamas gets down on his knees and cries]

The Footstool

MRS O'HARNESSEY You scarcely need to be told you owe me two years' digs money.

BARNEY How you do chide me.

MRS O'HARNESSEY I never pull my righteous punches.

BARNEY You look jaunty in those jodhpurs.

MRS O'HARNESSEY I don't feel it. The clinics don't want to buy my blood anymore.

Enter UNCLE CECIL Your blood?

BARNEY   The old geezers. She has a cellar full of them.

UNCLE CECIL   I know, I'm one of them. She makes us eat each other's testicles.

MRS O'HARNESSEY   Lies! Another of those fallacies of fascist folklore. Besides, Englishmen don't use them anymore.

BARNEY   I can imagine those baldy heads down there slobbering in a Golgotha of toothless mastication.

MRS O'HARNESSEY   [to Uncle Cecil] What are you doing here? I seem to remember Barney shooting you.

BARNEY   It was Ginger Jones I shot.

MRS O'HARNESSEY   In the back?

BARNEY   No, in the chest. He was running at me in a cowardly fashion.

MRS O'HARNESSEY   The important thing is, did you enjoy it?

BARNEY   Of course I did.

MRS O'HARNESSEY   It's better if you don't laugh though a thin, malicious smile is okay.

Enter HARRIET   Oh Barney, the man who shot Ginger Jones. How could I ever have doubted you. I'm sorry I knocked you down this morning.

BARNEY   That's alright, I was able to snap my jaw back into place.

HARRIET   He's my hero.

Somewhere

There's no reason why I can't be my own fallguy but I take exception to swimming out to the middle of this lake where Leamas is treading water in order to receive my orders, even the Big Boss doesn't make me do that.
   Talking of the Big Boss it's not all jam and Jerusalem with him neither.

THE BIG BOSS   Now listen carefully. Every week Mervyn Pratt gives a talk on Radio 4, when you hear him say "the man in the street does not know what's good for him" you spring into action. Got that?

BARNEY   Yes Big Boss, a Tinkerton has the fortitude even for that and knows his duty.

THE BIG BOSS   I want that made clear.
  [no harm in wanting, I always say]
It will be dangerous.

HARRIET   Don't let me stop you.

  [You won't believe what the fat cow does next.
  She brings out a wax phallus with a tiny hat like mine and a pair of specs, she flicks her lighter at the dummy prick]

HARRIET   I was a good little daddy's girl till I met you.

BARNEY   Your old da put Auntie Agnes in the pudding club and was a black sheep to boot. They didn't call him the swinging postman for nothing.

THE BIG BOSS   Higgins, I told you before, cut out the mixed metaphors.

Enter a JANE   [in a man's suit]   Be careful, Barney, don't lose your leg in Winnipeg.

  [I catch on quick. This is no ordinary Jane, it's

LOVELY MISS NIGHTINGALE   [whispering in my ear] Who do you think you're talking to?

BARNEY   [finding this whispering androgynously erotic] The Big Boss of course.

LOVELY MISS NIGHTINGALE   Don't you know a Blonde when you see one?

BARNEY   You don't mean….

  [I hope you weren't assuming the Big Boss was necessarily a man. That would never do]

THE BLONDE   Men are such fools.

BARNEY   Lies within lies like a Russian doll.

LOVELY MISS NIGHTINGALE   Some doll.

  [Next thing, Miss Lovely puts on her locker-room face]

THE BLONDE   [smiling]   Ma, she's making eyes at me.

LOVELY MISS NIGHTINGALE   [to the Blonde]   You can be my big boss if you want to.

HARRIET   [stamping on the smouldering phallus]   Fugh you, Higgins, I'm off to marry Jesus.

BARNEY   How will you know what he looks like, or am I missing the point?

HARRIET   As usual.

PART FIVE

The Footstool

Mrs O has called us sycophants together to find out who dug the pit that Auntie Atlas fell into last night.

MRS O'HARNESSEY   Come on Lord Spender, tell me you did it and you can have a stretcher of your own.

   [Entre nous it was me who dug it and covered it with branches to catch Clothilda's sly baggages coming up the beach with sailors. It wasn't meant for Auntie so I'm willing to send an innocent man to the pillory]

MRS O'HARNESSEY   [the cement on her face cracking maliciously] It's fin de siècle for you…Take him away
   [she says to the Ersatz Maids of Horror and Angst who escort the prisoner to her dungeon.
   Snag is, I'm the prisoner, not Lord Spender]

150
The dungeon

MRS O'HARNESSEY   Captain Moonlight, you are improperly dressed, the Ersatz Maids are complaining about your hairy legs.

BARNEY   [throwing my voice]   Wommanes conseil broghte us first to wo and made Adam fro paradys to go, ther as he was ful mury and wel at ese.

MRS O'HARNESSEY   [rearing up]   Who said that?

BARNEY   It was Chaucer, dear Matron, over there.

MRS O'HARNESSEY   I'll settle his hash
  [she says, pointing at the

SQUIRE   [hanging in a corner]   God speed the plough.

BARNEY   He's not himself. An unlettered and wayward ploughman exuding nothing more sinister than low nostalgia.

MRS O'HARNESSEY   Here's Dr Ragamuffin and Basher's Emergency Men to take you on deck.

[I should have mentioned that this particular dungeon is in an old prison hulk]

DR RAGAMUFFIN   No hard feelings?
   [I shake my head]
That is very good. I am seeing that you are a philosopher.

[Him and two nurses throw me overboard. I don't let the cold water get me down. I am after all a philosopher]

Billie's music hall

I trudge soakingly towards the hall. Billie strips me in her changing room. She puts TCP on my head where the nurses clobbered me. it hurts too.

BARNEY   I was abducted.

BILLIE   Poor dear, of course you were. Not those pesky Martians again, I hope.

[I am keeping a dignified silence when in bursts

MISS SUSIE   You have a fugitive here.
   [Billie and me look around]
It's Higgins.

BARNEY   Not me. I've paid my debt to Mrs O.

MISS SUSIE   Not here. Norfolk Island.
   [Enter her butler-husband]
Jeeves, tell Basher we need his Emergency Men again.

JEEVES   They might not arrest anyone in a pink dressing gown.

MISS SUSIE   'Course they will. They've all worked in care homes.
   [He exits, she calls after him]
And don't question my orders again.

BILLIE   I thought his name was Rupert.

MISS SUSIE   It was when we married. But after I spent all his money I just didn't feel the same about him. It was sad.

BILLIE You poor dear. At least you're over him now. No point in being maudlin.

MISS SUSIE [sighing] I'm bearing up as well as I can.

[And so am I. I've been in tighter spots, like when Harriet found me buying Ester rums and blackcurrants in the Seven Stars]

BILLIE What's he done to deserve Norfolk Island?

MISS SUSIE He tied up Harriet as a tethered goat in Alimonia. Amelia saw him do it.

[Eyewitnesses! What about the poor criminals who are wrongly convicted on account of them. Though I suppose it balances out the crimes they get away with]

MISS SUSIE They'll sort him out on the island. The cadre has been reinforced by two drill sergeants bordering on sadistic lunacy.

BARNEY Are there any other type?

Norfolk Island

Uncle Cecil and me are guinea pigs on a course for would-be widows. I see him singing to himself in his native Cossack, a single tear comes to his eye.

BARNEY   Sometimes I think you're not all there.

Enter DR RAGAMUFFIN   I am being the judge of that.
   [He places his stethoscope against Uncle Cecil's forehead] This is jolly good. Very fine to take his part as a subject in the trial.

   [And off he goes, looking at his Rolex]

UNCLE CECIL   Oh Barney, I'm just a merry begotten simple body and I don't deserve this.

BARNEY   Don't worry, every clown has a simple lining. But anyone wearing plus fours and a deerstalker deserves all they get.

A VOICE   Nice dump you've got here
   [shouts Bernard Holland, inviting himself in with a baseball bat. He bangs Uncle Cecil on the back of his legs and he jerks around like a

puppet on a string.

But that's as far as Bernard Holland gets. In comes my squad of Ancient Mariners. They're cross because they're sober and they give him a right good thumping.

Give me the fools and I will finish the job]

The Footstool

MRS O'HARNESSEY   You have done well, Captain Moonlight. Norfolk Island is now almost in my power. I truly believe that sometimes you know what you're doing.

BARNEY   Yes, and there's usually more than one prong to my plans.

MRS O'HARNESSEY   Insinuating those ruffians of yours was particularly clever.

BARNEY   I divide my Ancient Mariners into three detachments: the shock troop, the cannon fodder and the forlorn hope, all equal in my eyes and all getting the same grub.

MRS O'HRNESSEY   That's very fair minded of you....Yes, indeed, I'll teach this Horace Himmler to make secret weapons on the island without telling me.

BARNEY   Uncle Cecil's life was in my hands as I insinuated him past the mines and electric wire. But for you, my succulent siren, I laugh at danger.

MRS O'HARNESSEY   I'm glad to know that because you must go back. Getting rid of one rogue may release an even bigger one….
   And another thing, my hero, you've been making time with that tramp again. Against my orders.

BARNEY   She said she needed someone to keep her warm at night.

MRS O'HARNESSEY   You leave that dog alone.

BARNEY   Yes, Matron, her mushy thighs and overripe bum will no longer lead me into temptation.

MRS O'HARNESSEY   Are you really that hard up? I never heard of you sleeping with your wife before.

You too can have a body like Harriet.
   If you're not careful.

MRS GRUNDY   That's not nice. Women get plumper every year.

   [Mrs O has a cheek telling me manners. I mean, that's rich coming from a woman who bricked up her poor husband behind the wall]

MRS GRUNDY   I expect she got the idea from you.

BARNEY   Yes, I once bricked the wife up in the cellar. Dear Harriet, she does so take things to heart. That's what bricklayers do.

MRS GRUNDY   Watch out for the mad bricklayer.

   [Talk of the devil, here she comes now with the priest]

HARRIET   The Father says he's dying to meet you after all these years.

THE PRIEST   We have a lot to talk about.

   [Smiles and sugar, just another way of telling lies. Priests are like

Japanese. You can be with them for ages and never know what they're really thinking. I expect there are conflicts under the surface.

I don't mind them holding hands but I won't stand for kissing on the lips]

Clothilda drops in to remind me I'm still working for her. I can expect trouble seeing as how I haven't been on the case. So I put on my false nose and tache and go to the door before she knocks it down.

CLOTHILDA   Oh hello, I don't think we've met. I'm looking for that idle bastard Higgins.

BARNEY   As a matter of fact---

[This is all I get to say as my cheeks are being squeezed together in that trademark grip of hers]

CLOTHILDA   When the Gentleman Caller advised me to hire a Tinkerton I expected to get something for my money.

[The Gentleman Caller? *You* know. He's in the West Ham Intercity Book of Quotations with Where there's honey, there's bees, Miss

Nancy.

  He's a burglar and he doesn't care who knows it since the Plod don't bother anymore. There's been talk the Girl Guides will be drafted in but they're already stretched trying to shore up our borders.

  As for Clothilda for all her famous grips, I just view her as a machine for turning puddings and pies into something else, but a Tinkerton does like to be of some help to his clients]

BARNEY   I have something for you. Portuguese Joe is a spy.

CLOTHILDA   Who's he spying for?

BARNEY   For me.

CLOTHILDA   I always knew he was up to no good.

BARNEY   I have my tentacles everywhere.

  [You see this detective business. Sometimes I take it seriously but mainly it's a front. Don't get me wrong, I'm not saying I couldn't have been good at it. I could walk into any detective agency in the country and how many can say they've been in the *News of the World*]

CLOTHILDA   You go back to keeping watch over my smugglers and strumpets and no slacking off this time.

   [It takes a strong man to stand in a rainy field all night with his arms out disguised as a scarecrow and once was enough.
   But I don't tell Clothilda that. Not as long as she's holding my gooseberries]

One of the most famous heroes of all time was Higgins the Hammer who took his knights to France where in a valley inaccessible to men of straw he rescued from nightriders a certain Mrs Grundy and restored to her all her husband's gold teeth offered up to Madame Mao when he was in a fever.

MRS GRUNDY   I don't know what to think.

MADAME MAO   Higgins, say nothing to your fellow time-travellers but Monmouth has been taken.

   [I love it when she's historical]

THE CRUSHER   Hey nonny no, hey nonny no.

It's difficult to feel sorry for the Crusher even if he does have a ring through his nose. He's crawled back into his cardboard kennel and is snarling at

LOVELY MISS NIGHTINGALE   Just cop a plea and then Matron and Billie will stop poking you.

THE CRUSHER   I left my confession in my other kennel.

BARNEY   I think he likes it.

   [he starts to bark]

LOVELY MISS NIGHTINGALE   Will no-one rid me of this turbulent hound?

MATRON   I shall call him Becket.

A VOICE   And I shall call you my main suspect
   [declares Uncle Cecil, lassoing Matron and deftly reeling her in]
Come on, duckie, I arrested you a year ago and forgot to take you in.
   [Becket catches his eye]
Where's his lead?

LOVELY MISS NIGHTINGALE   Leave him alone, you dogsnatcher.

MATRON   [taking advantage of his short attention span] Uncle Cecil, why don't you take me for a stroll through the stubble?

UNCLE CECIL   Don't mind if I do, dear lady.

   [And off they go hand in hand to drink stout in the Seven Stars]

Drabtown races

Harriet has a job as a steward.

MRS O'HARNESSEY   [to Harriet] That Amelia has two entries, it's against the rules.

HARRIET   Rules are for fools.

BARNEY   Some steward.

HARRIET I'm only human, you know. How could I refuse dear Amelia when she frowned at me in such an enticing way.

MRS O'HARNESSEY We'll see about that
  [she exclaims and strides off, bold as a bully, her short skirt showcasing the splendour of her treetrunk thighs]

HARRIET [standing there with her mouth open] I hope I know what we are doing.

BARNEY I'm in a tight spot alright.

HARRIET Be strong, Barney, and cut all sentimental ties with your horrible former self.

BARNEY Mrs O said her treatment would break new grounds and I would learn a lot. So she sat me down with a cigar and a bag of crisps and put me in the magnetic coil.

HARRIET You always were a great man for learning, what with your encyclopaedias, microscopes and horoscopes.

BARNEY Snag is, the treatment brainwashed me to always do as she says.

HARRIET So now you're a prawn.

[I nod sorrowfully. The lady jockeys arrive. The whistle goes. My sore back is killing me and my heart is chugging like a train.
I feel the crop to spur me on. I make it to the finish. It's only one hundred yards but it's a hot day. I lower myself to let my rider dismount. Breathless as I am, I admire her bumtight leggings and clinging sweat-soaked teeshirt.

The Footstool's cellar

MATRON [sitting by the fire, roasting Sleepy Sid's chestnuts] This'll learn me not to trust little rats again.

[I'm down here too. I'm in a bunker behind a bookcase beyond the boulders at the back of the basement. Helping Matron is a Sibyl wearing a hat with a veil]

SIBYL That's where noblesse oblige gets you.

LADY JANE GREY I know what you mean. I'd hardly sat down before they came and took me away.

MATRON   Nothing personal. I owed Cousin Henry one.
   [Is she off her rocker or am I?
   Don't answer that]
If it makes you feel better come and rake your nails [looks down at Sleepy Sid] along this boss-backed toad.

SIBYL   Sounds like fun. I don't like the look of this Higgins. Can I take him home with me?

MATRON   He's not for sale. But you can rent him.

SIBYL   No, rehabilitating criminals is a waste of time.

   [I hear a cranking sound like that of the Tardis. The Pyramid appears out of nowhere.
   Many voices sigh as one.

Aaagh….Uncle Cecil

CHORUS   Wherever I see the U.C sign, the U.C sign, always fine, wherever I see the U.C sign, I want to make him mine.

   [Yes, it's the Sultanas stepping out of the Pyramid]

BARNEY   It's bad enough you taking the Pyramid without permission but it wasn't built to carry around big girls like that.

UNCE CECIL   I couldn't rescue you without it. The coppers have closed all roads indefinitely because a car ran into a dog.

BARNEY   Why do they do that?

CHIEF WOODENTOP   Because we can.

LADY JANE GREY   Why is it a criminal offence to hurt the feelings of certain people?

CHIEF WOODENTOP   Ask me another.

Dockland

Listen to the chemist from Cologne telling the Misses Marble in melodious German:

ESTER   Sie are now sausage meat.

MISSES MARBLE   Oh deary me, we don't mean to be old.

BARNEY   Calm down, you nebbing old biddies, it's only her teutonic way of trying to sell you face cream with hormones in it.

   [Here comes

FRANCIS THE TALKING MULE   Who's this tart on my back prodding me with an umbrella?

TART   I'm Jean the Baptist.

   [News to me the Baptist wears a hat with flowers on it and a long nineteen century velvet dress.
   And to cap it all here comes some noodles singing the Monster Mash]

In darkest dockland down a moon-lit alley there's a flop joint called the Star Chamber.
   Harriet's wearing a tight black number split up the sides like the armchair she's filling. She's watching the Crusher take out his dick.

HARRIET Stop waving that thing at me. You know very well you're one of those. So stop it.

BARNEY Whatever are you at?

HARRIET I'm making some money. But not from the likes of him. He hasn't 2d to rub together.

BARNEY Don't come the poor mouth. I give what I can afford and you've never had to take in washing.

HARRIET Take in washing! In your book that means everything is okay?

   [There's a former client of mine called Baldy Neill. Harriet goes over and strokes his face]

HARRIET You needn't be ashamed of being here, you know. We have our own curate on the premises and one or two nurses. And we're all married women too. To keep it respectable. I do think single girls should be more careful. Don't you think so too?

BALDY NEILL Most considerate of you. But when does the show start?

HARRIET   In a wee while. I think you'll find it quite avant garde.

BALDY NEILL   But not pointless?

HARRIET   Oh yes, it can be pointless if that's what you like.

   [We look up as a tall blonde approaches in a determined manner]

VERA VAMP   My client informs me that you refused her a position here, saying she wasn't up to theatrical standards. But that wasn't the case, was it?

HARRIET   She's just playing the discrimination card.

BARNEY   People play a lot of cards nowadays.

   [Harriet clocks her one. They fall to the floor and start wrassling. After a bit the wife slaps the floor]

VERA VAMP   [examining her stockings for ladders] I'll be sending you a letter.

   [After she leaves a copper enters and says to Harriet

CONSTABLE   Reason to believe you're keeping a disorderly house here.

HARRIET   Ha! This is nothing, you want to see my house after he's been there a few days
   [she exclaims, looking at me]

Here's Harriet leaving the courthouse with a wind-blown umbrella partly covering her face. I haven't the heart to tell her there are no photographers. She's not quite at the Cynthia Payne standard yet.

The music hall

Brutality Jones has taken over from Billie but has fallen down one of the trapdoors on the stage for acts that get booed.

BRUTALITY JONES   [on a stretcher, to Lord Spender]   I'm on the way out but keep the rabble coming in.

   [I line up the staff]

BARNEY I'm the gaffer here now. Keep a look out for troublemakers and be particularly rough on rats like Ginger Jones

[I go for a drink in Billie's Bar, pushing my way through barhounds and B-girls in diaphanous drawers showing off their belly whiskers, trying to persuade punters to buy them whisky which comes out of a Brooke Bond packet]

BARNEY [to chief B-girl] I won't have my punters cheated, which is why I'm banning tea and what is that metal monster doing behind the bar?

CHIEF B-GIRL It's called a computer. Her nibs put it there to project three dimensional images of....

BARNEY Of what?

CHIEF B-GIRL Take a look.

[There's a flash of scarlet as she flicks a finger and the next thing I see is the Waist rising like a whale from the depths of the future]

THE WAIST I am the ghost of a flabby neutered England.

[Barney Higgins, says I to myself, you're spellbound again as the Waist leads me through the bodies English hanging like game among cobwebs.

It's not particularly poignant to see a fat man cry]

The Footstool

MRS O'HARNESSEY   Barney, wouldn't it be better if you told me where the Pyramid is.

[I've never been keen on this sharing concept but I do like the way she delicately hikes up her skirt when she crosses her legs.
To the acclaim of Tom, Dick and Harry.
Who? They're the new Untouchables, born again into the Footstool, begotten into priapism and defilement from which they can never escape, their only purpose to show constant appreciation of Mrs O's womanly figure.

MRS O'HARNESSEY   Alright, boys, work Higgins over, he's only hisself to blame.

[But there's a problem. She's kept them on drugs, permanently aroused and with little grub so it's not difficult to smite them down and leave them twitching]

MRS O'HARNESSEY…I knew you could do it.

Enter HARRIET   He's my hero.

Miss Wink's Private Asylum

Where I am a day patient.
  I go in by the window.

UNCLE CECIL   What's wrong with the door?

BARNEY   Because you boobytrapped it, that's why.

UNCLE CECIL   [giggling]   Can't you take a joke?

BARNEY   What's that red stuff on your spectacles?

Enter THE DUKE'S WEAK SISTER   [fluttering her blouse]
My lipstick. He wanted wet kisses.

BARNEY   [to Uncle Cecil] Couldn't you have taken them off first?

UNCLE CECIL   I have my dignity to consider.

Enter THE SQUIRE   I lost mine on the prison balconies of Balbriggin.

UNCLE CECIL   Dirty old moonraker.

THE DUKE'S WEAK SISTER   You can't talk. Happy valleys are all the same to you.

Here comes

HARRIET THE HOUSEKEEPER   Attention, attention, all youse ones face the wall now.

   [There's the sound of Mozart, that's the mad violin quartet next door. They wear masks but I recognise the legs.
   All this means Quean Victoria is passing by. She affects the Alexandran Limp to tantalize the Squire but like the rest of the lower

castes he's not allowed to look. But he has Harriet's permission to think about it while it lasts]

THE SQUIRE   My nanny was a limping lady and I've been infatuated ever since.

HARRIET THE HOUSEKEEPER   This here, your majesty, is where we keep the incomplete headcases. We call it the Lunatic Fringe.

QUEAN VICTORIA   This one here, why's he wearing short trousers?

BARNEY   Not my idea---

HARRIET THE HOUSEKEEPER   Shut it! [she shoves a handkerchief in my mouth] This one's going to public school where they starve and beat them and turn out deeply flawed men who become incompetent generals and timeservers at the House of Lords.

BARNEY   I'm quite flawed enough alweady, dank you.

QUEAN VICTORIA   Tell him to pull his socks up.

HARRIET THE HOUSEKEEPER   You heard, Higgins. Right up to the knee.

[A mere glimpse of the goings-on in the asylum before Quean Victoria is led back to her room, and don't you hear echoes of Spenser's Fairie Queen in this saga of eloquence and sorrowful seclusion?

No, neither do I]

The Ruins

ESTER   Dat Pyramid, by ze Prushuns it vas invented. Zat is how to ze moon ve vent.

[True enough, when the Americans landed they found empty lager bottles]

A VOICE   I worked on it meself
   [says Uncle Cecil stepping out of his grandfathers clock]
You didn't know I was a slave labourer, did you?

ESTER   Ve call it Die Nemesis.

   [Lady Betty who is a figurehead for the Way of the Arch has sent me

on a mission. Lady Betty (I'm allowed this intimacy as part of my conditioning) can see no good in the chemist from Cologne.
 What I can see are two voluptuous thighs as she stands above my head which is attached to a magnetic coil. This is me being recharged.
 Uncle Cecil crawls across the room]

ESTER   Nein, nein du kanst not be mein doormat today.
 [he's always pestering women when he has a drop taken]
 Nein, nein, I vill not let you on my bed ov nails lie.

[You see how strange he is. Not like me. I'm not the sort to annoy quiet folk, I'm just another unsung sidekick with a natural interest in the private fabrics of lady skaters as they burl round and round. What say you, doctor, am I right in the head?]

DOCTOR RAGAMUFFIN   London belongs to me.

[You see, he's not right neither. But that didn't stop him putting one of Uncle Cecil's Sultanas up the duff.
 The old fool makes a run at him. Ester puts out a foot, over he goes]

DOCTOR RAGAMUFFIN   He will be bunged in with Sleepy Sid.

UNCLE CECIL   Oubliettes should be single occupancy only according to the Jennifer convention.

BARNEY   Always the changing room lawyer
   [I remark as I take off the coil and go over to Dr Ragamuffin who is now trying to examine the wife's tits]
Take your hands offa her, she's bad enough with her nerves as it is.

HARRIED   My saviour!

BARNEY   You may talk of Mrs Grundy and other famous wives but I would not swop my Harriet Brigid Higgins for any of them. Or whatever you name is.

   [I'm buttering her up because happiness is a cigar called

HARRIET   It's funny how quickly I can change from being an old bag into an object of desire.

BARNEY   You are my Elizabeth and I am your Essex.

HARRIET   How romantic you are. I always know when your floosies are giving you the cold shoulder. What's the matter, stopped giving them presents, have you?

[She's right for once. You may have noticed I haven't pulled off any jobs lately]

A road in Dockland

HARRIET You won't find me scrubbing parsnips in vicarages.

BARNEY That's not the point. You'll be looking for a lead.

HARRIET What's a lead look like?

BARNEY You won't know till you find one.

HARRIET I don't do vacuuming neither.

BARNEY So I've noticed.

HARRIET Why can't you leave those poor clergymen alone?

BARNEY Because Vic is a fence and we need to know where the goods go so we can cut him out, see? The first thing is to go through his personal files.

HARRIET No good. His wife would do that regular.

BARNEY Quite right. I wasn't thinking.

HARRIET Stop hopping about.

BARNEY I'm not hopping. I'm jumping.
   [After reading about Spring-heeled Jack I invented a pair of jumping boots]
This is only the prototype. Once I power them with petrol I will be uncatchable.

HARRIET Oh Barney, I'll never doubt you again.

BARNEY How I think them up, I don't know.

HARRIET You'll never have to worry about rozzers no more.

BARNEY That's right. I'll take over rackets here and start up rackets there, where there have been none before.

HARRIET   You'll be unstoppable.

BARNEY   I'll get a real gun. Stick 'em up, I'll say. Or, Reach for the sky. I've always wanted to say that….

　[We reach the church]

Two days later

There's no excuse for Harriet taking up with the vicar. Only last year I bought her a music-centre so she could stay at home more. She liked to dance to swing music and piano rock. Sometimes I'd even dance with her myself. How many husbands can say that?

My office

Sleepy Sid has no business wanting a sex change even though it's all the fashion. After he hurries off to have his penis caned this poppet comes in, voluptuously settles in the visitor's chair. I look up from filling my pipe, try to place those kissable legs.

Then it comes to me. I know her from Norfolk Island.

BARNEY   You're in radio, aren't you
   [I remark, noticing the mike sticking out of her handbag]

POPPET   You a mindreader or what? What's that in your pocket?

BARNEY   It's only Pythagoras, my ferret.

POPPET   You are funny.

BARNEY   Really, it is.

POPPET   I believe you.

   [Who could forget being tied hand and foot to a bed on a frozen lake while this poppet in a short skirt makes circuits round your erect penis with the palm of her hand?
   Only the mind of a Miss Susie could think of such a thing. She's the poppet I'm telling you about. I'll have to watch myself if she's recording me. She doesn't know I know.

MISS SUSIE   It must be wonderful being the detective who

discovered the Pyramid.

BARNEY   I have my moments.

MISS SUSIE   You discovered the Holy Kettle too, didn't you?

BARNEY   Yes, when I went among tinkers on the Barbary Coast.

MISS SUSIE   And you found the earliest draft of the Book of Amazement.

BARNEY   I know an Ancient Semite when I see one, he was last seen in Brussels in 1884.

MISS SUSIE   So why was Mrs O'Harnessey, Lady Betty and Amelia all using you as a dogsbody?

   [You might say certain temptresses overcame the remnants of my self-respect or that I was blackmailed or that it was sore but I liked it.
   Or you mightn't want to say anything.
   Very well, if you're going to be like that, I'll just tell you those great dames were enemies and each of them hired me to spy on the others]

BARNEY   Let's just say not all is what it seems.

MISS SUSIE   I knew there had to be something. My editor on the programme thinks you're a modern day Walter Raleigh.

BARNEY   Really? What's her name?

MISS SUSIE   Josephine Stark.

BARNEY   [taken back] She's been betraying this country for years.

MISS SUSIE   That doesn't matter at the BBC. She fits in well with our culture of bias, opinionation, nepotism and of course she is, like all of us, grossly overpaid.

   [Just one carriage of the Gravy Train]

BARNEY   I suppose it figures. She always wanted to make a name for herself.

MISS STARK   What name was that?

BARNEY   I'm not au fait with her vocabulary.

MISS SUSIE   Yes she does have a slight lisp but our sensitive young men adore her.

[She sees me glancing at her handbag. She edges it under the desk. I'm hoping she doesn't notice Sleepy Sid who has crawled under it]

But back to you, Barney, our listeners would be interested in your adventures with the Pyramid. I take it you have it parked somewhere safe.

[Entre nous, it's at a place called Eye of the Needle. There's a few wild ponies milling about but I haven't seen any camels go through it.
But I wouldn't. Major Peppar (aka Leamas) has been prowling around it recently. Only last night he shot my hat off.

[The doorbell rings]

SLEEPY SID   Avon calling, Avon calling
[he cries, pushing up on the desk in his excitement. This releases Pythagoras my ferret. He dives into her handbag. Miss Susie picks it up and walks out]

Miss Wink's Private Asylum

Poor Sleepy Sid scurrying about, bent over, with one mad eye. He's been confined for stealing from handbags. He likes used lipstick, imagines it moving across pursed lady-like lips.

   Dr Ragamuffin gave Nursey a new chemical cosh. It says on the bottle: To be well shaken. After Sleepy swallowed it she and the Crusher each took a leg and an arm and gave him a right rattle.

   I'm in because I talk to walls. I told him nothing's said about those Hebrews who talk to the Wailing Wall, but you can't talk to psychiatrists, they think they know more about you than you do yourself.

NURSEY   You can call me Matron
   [she says from somewhere in the region of two large orbs which just happen to catch my eye]
But it'll cost you.

   [I call her Keyhole Kate because she's always spying on me. She's quite bald, you know, under that wig and she's not particular about changing her linen (so rumour has it) and I'm not at all interested in her chunky thighs encased in fully-fashioned stockings]

BARNEY   The last time I called you Matron you tied a rope around my testicles, an unusual way to begin therapy, I thought at the time.

Then you injected me and it was all I could do to stand upright. I could hardly walk.

NURSEY   So? I helped you, didn't I?

BARNEY   Yes to be fair you did. You pulled me behind you with the rope. And what a view I had.

   [There was no linen under that thin white uniform – just as long as you know]

NURSEY   Miss Wink says you are ready for the anomaly.

BARNEY   What?

MISS WINK   [entering] Anomalies are idiosyncratic situations contrary to normal practice. In such instances a mere slip of a girl like Nursey may control a big important man.

BARNEY   I'd hardly call her a mere slip.

NURSEY   I heard that. Oh Miss Wink, if it wasn't for my Christian fortitude I don't know what I'd do.

MISS WINK   It sustains us all my dear. With notable exceptions
   [she says and I feel the force of her gaze through the fabric of her veil]
If only he'd *believe*.

NURSEY   He told me he's a hitman called the Slasher and you'd never know where he'd slash next.

MISS WINK   That's him all over. Last week he was a private eye called Captain Moonlight.

NURSEY   That's right, miss, with his mail-order detective kit and dummy gun. He thinks this isolation chamber is his office.

MISS WINK   Time for his injection.

Wait till you hear this.

One year later.

I'm back in my office. Mrs O tracked me down. I always said landladies would make good detectives. I made up the money

I owed her by becoming a pavement artist.

   My eye catches the egg-timer that holds Harriet's ashes. It's in a pride of place on the window sill. I do miss her. She kept me on my toes. But I still think that a married man can not be his true self. He compromises too much. Still, them were days.

   This frail comes in. She moves slowly up to my desk. Her eyes hint at a bargain her soft lips might keep, yet she looks hesitant, shy and only slightly sinful like kisses in a cathedral.

   A jingle comes on the radio. Cyril Lord, Cyril Lord, this is luxury you can afford.

THE FRAIL   I'm expecting a little parcel from Paris.

   [She goes over to my bookshelf, looks at the sign:
Please do not ask for the lend of books as a poke in the eye often offends.
Her shoulders start to shake. I can't tell if she's laughing or crying]

That's my story and I'm sticking to it.

The end of another play
by
Barney Higgins

If you enjoyed this there's more on Amazon - Books.

Regards,
Barney Higgins
aka
Bill Magill
Bournemouth

Printed in Great Britain
by Amazon